Christy's Senior Year

Maud Johnson

SCHOLASTIC INC.
New York Toronto London Auckland Sydney Tokyo

ISBN 0-590-33097-7

12 11 10 9 8 7 6 5 4 3 2 1   9   4 5 6 7 8 9/8

Printed in the U.S.A.   06

Christy's Senior Year

A Wildfire® Book

One

Some memories are good and cause you to smile, but some are painful, the way a raw sore or a burn can be painful. It was the hurting kind of memories that swirled through me as I stepped off the school bus at Greenview High the first Monday morning in March. Other students milled about, some of them seniors as I was. I spoke to everyone, but my voice sounded flat and mechanical.

Mike had been dead for almost two months, but it was a fresh jolt all five mornings a week not to find him waiting for me at school as he'd done before, leaning against a corner of the building with his books resting on his left hip. He would grin when he saw me, and a surge of warmth and love for him would flow through my body. Usually he said, "Hi there, Christy," and I'd answer, "Hi, yourself," even though he and I hadn't needed words to communicate. We would look into each other's eyes and smile because being together was wonderful and —

I caught myself sharply, forcing my thoughts away from the past, making myself return to the present.

Mike Maxwell was gone. Dead. He would never again wait for me at school or come to my house or put his arms around me and kiss me. He was the boy I'd loved deeply, still loved and still ached to be near, and he had died in January from injuries he'd received in a New Year's Eve car accident.

As I entered school on that cold, blustery March Monday, I told myself for the millionth time since Mike's death that I had my emotions under control, something that was partly true and partly a fib. At least those emotions were under control on the surface, and I didn't break down in public.

Don't think about Mike, don't think about Mike, I ordered myself silently and started down the long school corridor.

For a second I wasn't sure I'd heard my name spoken. My mind had been full of personal thoughts, and the hall was noisy with students chattering and laughing on the way to their lockers and homerooms.

"Christy. Christy Jamison!"

The voice belonged to a man and it came from behind me. That time there was no mistaking the words. I turned to find Mr. Brady, principal of Greenview High, motioning to me from the doorway leading into his office.

2

A girl I'd never seen before was with him. Dressed in jeans with a white shirt and a sleeveless yellow suede vest, she had short blond hair that curled softly around a very pretty face. A blue tweed coat was slung over her arm, and she carried a blue shoulder bag and a looseleaf notebook. I retraced my steps, pausing beside the two of them.

"Christy, this is Nina Farrell," Mr. Brady said. "Nina, Christy Jamison. You girls have something in common because both of you are seniors and newcomers to Virginia. Or rather, Christy was a newcomer last year. I've assigned Nina to your homeroom, Christy, and Mrs. Perkins is expecting her. Will you take her upstairs to two eighteen? I'm needed in the office."

Saying I'd be glad to do it, I exchanged smiles with Nina, instantly seeing myself as I'd been fifteen months earlier when my family moved to the small town of Greenview, Virginia, in sight of the Blue Ridge Mountains.

It wasn't that Nina Farrell and I had identical features or similar coloring, because we didn't. My brown hair was a contrast to her lovely blondeness, and my figure, I realized ruefully, lacked a lot of the curves hers had. She didn't seem as shy as I was fifteen months earlier, but it was the first day in new surroundings for her and I understood what that meant. On my first day at Greenview High, I was so tense my stomach felt as if it was filled with hard little stones.

Nina wasn't as tense as I'd been my first day — or she didn't seem to be — but I tried to reassure her, just the same. "You'll like Greenview," I said. "I do. The people are great once you get to know them, and the mountains are beautiful."

"I'm already impressed with the scenery," she answered, and smiled again.

"Where did you move from?"

"Ohio. What about you, Christy?"

"We came here from New York State and we'd lived there less than two years when Dad was sent to Virginia. I wasn't eager to move again quickly, but now I'm glad we did."

If we hadn't come to Greenview, I'd never have known Mike.

Without telling Nina what I was thinking, I said aloud, "I was a junior last year and the move was hard for me, but it must be even more of a grind for you to change schools in the final semester of your senior year."

"I grant you it wasn't my choice. You win some and you lose some." She laughed as she spoke, and I had the impression she was making the best of the situation. "Anyhow, here I am. It wasn't my idea to leave Ohio right now, but in one way I guess it was good."

Her last comment made me curious, and I waited for her to explain. When she didn't, I let the subject drop. Nina and I had known one another only ten minutes, and it would have been hard for me to pump her with questions.

4

"Here's the library." I gestured toward a pair of double doors on the right. "The gym is under it in the basement, and the auditorium and cafeteria are at the back at the far end of the building. All the science labs and the home ec department are on the third floor — no elevators, so be prepared to hike. Did Mr. Brady give you a class schedule and tell you the number of your bus? The buses leave school ten minutes after the dismissal bell and the drivers won't wait."

"A class schedule, yes. But I'll put my feet on the pavement instead of rating a bus ride. Mom and I have an apartment on Harrison Street just five blocks from school."

The reference to her new address startled me, and I didn't know why. My only connection with Harrison Street was that David Webster, a boy I hadn't known long, lived there, and I felt disloyal to Mike for thinking about another guy even casually.

In my silence, Nina had dug into her purse for the schedule card and now handed it to me.

"You and I have the same English and math classes," I said, checking the card as we climbed the stairs. "I'll warn you about Mr. Hansen, the math teacher. He's famous for giving pop quizzes. We're in the same final study hall, too. Our lunch hours are different, though. I eat during the first one and you have the second. Maybe we'll pass someone I know who has the second and — Oh, there's Kim Clark."

Kim, also a senior, joined us when I called to her, and I introduced the two girls. Kim, quiet and studious, hadn't dated much until recently. She and Bud Warren, a friend of Mike's, "discovered" each other, despite having been classmates since elementary school. When Kim and Bud were together, she was positively radiant and he seemed to be floating on the clouds.

After explaining to Kim that Nina was new, I mentioned lunch and Kim got the message. "Nina, I'll wait for you outside the cafeteria door," she said. "I have to dash now because I need to stop at my locker before the bell rings. See you later."

Kim hurried up the stairs ahead of us, and Nina gave me a grateful glance. "You're a love, Christy," she said softly. "I was dreading lunch."

"Don't forget that I know exactly how it is," I nodded. "I've been new."

I wanted to spare her what I'd endured at lunchtime on my initial day at Greenview High. When I arrived at school that first morning, Mr. Brady asked a girl named Emily Halstead, a senior, to take me to my homeroom. She seemed friendly, and at noon as I went down the cafeteria line, I spotted her at a table and took a seat beside her — or tried to do it.

She gave me an icy look as I set my tray on the table and she announced that while there were no assigned seats in the cafeteria, only seniors "liked" that particular table — her voice as acid as if my being a junior made me guilty of a crime. I gulped in dismay and apologized, my face rosy. I'd unintentionally made a spectacle of myself.

Feeling dreadfully self-conscious, I stood there by Emily a second, trying to determine if I'd be less conspicuous moving to another table and perhaps having to endure a similar remark from other students or sticking it out where I was for that one meal. Going would be better, I decided, glancing at the set of Emily's jaw. My appetite had been completely killed at that point.

A girl named Betsy Collins, a junior and someone I'd noticed in a couple of my morning classes, was at the next table and had overheard what Emily said. Betsy motioned me to an empty seat next to her, and I could have hugged her. Later she became my best friend in Greenview — except for Mike, of course. Betsy and Gordon Sager had often double-dated with Mike and me.

That March Monday was a routine school day for me. Nina and I waved to each other when we passed in the hall, and, just as I anticipated, Mr. Hansen gave one of his pop quizzes, on a Monday, no less. Miss Dannell, my history teacher, announced a big test for Friday, ignoring the collective groans and sighs echoing around the classroom.

At noon I ate lunch with Betsy, Gordon, and Bud Warren, as always. Mike used to eat there, too, and all of us had learned to ignore his vacant seat. I didn't know if other students refused to use that chair out of respect for him or possibly for me since they knew I'd been Mike's girl. I couldn't bring myself to mention it, even though I hated the constant reminder that Mike was gone.

The four of us gabbed a few minutes before I said, "Have you met Nina Farrell?" — my gaze moving around the table to include everybody. "She's from Ohio and she seems nice."

"You mean the blonde?" Gordon rolled his eyes, then winked at Betsy. "Wow and double wow! I go for the type."

"Down, boy." Betsy patted him on the head as if he were a big dog. "You can look at blondes all you want, but doing more than looking and saying hello is a giant no-no."

"Gee, Mom, I'm a big boy now," he teased. "I brush my own teeth and tie my own shoelaces and button my own buttons. But I've never, ever, dated a blonde."

Gordon grinned at her and everybody at the table laughed. Betsy took his cracks in stride.

"Oh, yes, you have," she retaliated. "I'm a blonde. Didn't you know? You must be color-blind not to have realized it."

That brought fresh laughter, as Betsy had black hair. When she and Gordon kidded like that, I felt a familiar tug at my heart because Mike and I used to have the same sort of silly give-and-take conversations. I missed them just as I missed everything else about Mike.

"You people be nice to Nina," I urged. "You've lived here in Greenview forever and you don't know about moving or being new. Nina is really sweet and she needs friends."

"Doesn't everybody?" Bud mumbled from the end of the table, so serious that three pairs of eyes looked in his direction. He wasn't a big talker but he could put a lot into a few words.

"Don't worry about her, Christy." Gordon was instantly as serious as Bud sounded. "If she's as nice as you say she is, she'll make friends. Before school is over today, she'll probably have a different date lined up for every night this week."

"Big deal!" Betsy interrupted. "You guys won't be able to wait to get in the locker room and brag and compare notes on her!"

"What do you mean by 'you guys'?" Gordon said. "I thought you and I were going steady. I have no intention of dating Nina."

"You know what I mean, Gordon. A new girl is a challenge to most guys and I think it's gross. Okay, I was wrong to lump *you* in that group, but don't deny the locker room talk."

He stared at her until she looked ill at ease. "How do you know what goes on in the guys' locker room?" he persisted.

"Girls know. Everyone knows."

"You mean to say you never talk about us? Aw, come on, Betsy," Gordon returned.

"We don't keep score the way you boys do," she said defiantly.

9

There was an edge to both their voices, and what had begun as a simple conversation was turning into a word duel. To break it up before they began fussing, I announced that Kim was eating lunch with Nina, and at the mention of Kim's name something wonderful happened to Bud. The corners of his mouth turned up and his eyes softened.

"I know what Christy means about making friends," Betsy commented, her tone natural once more.

"Spread the info around," Bud said. "I haven't the foggiest idea what you're talking about."

"You males probably can't understand, but some girls hate to be near a beautiful girl," Betsy explained. "Not Kim, obviously, and not Christy, since they're being extra special nice to Nina. I don't think I fall into the I-hate-beautiful-girls group, either. At least, I hope I don't. It's a form of jealousy, I guess. A person as gorgeous as Nina makes the rest of us seem awfully plain by comparison, and that's one reason Jill gets along better with guys than she does with females. Nina is just as good-looking as Jill Rogers in my book, and she may have to face the same situation Jill faces because of it."

The last thing I wanted was a discussion of Jill Rogers. Betsy seldom talked about people unless she was paying them compliments, and she'd lowered her voice to avoid being overheard beyond our table when she referred to Jill. But the cafeteria was one of the most public spots at Greenview High, and, at that moment, Jill was seated about twenty feet from us, her tinkling laughter rising occasionally above the chatter.

Jill, with her gold-flecked auburn hair and her perfect figure, had been known as Mike Maxwell's girl at the time my family moved to Virginia. I had been disappointed, since I had been drawn to Mike from the first time I ever saw him, although I was too shy to let him know. I'd daydreamed about him, never daring to think he and I would be more than casual friends. The miracle happened in April of the previous year. After he and Jill broke up, he began dating me.

Jill wasn't stupid, but she didn't study enough to receive decent grades. In addition to her beauty, she possessed the ability to attract boys with little apparent effort on her part, and Betsy was correct in saying Jill got along better with guys than she did with girls. As much as I loathed admitting it to myself, there were moments when I, too, had been jealous of Jill Rogers.

That part of my life ended with Mike's death, but I felt as though I'd explode if the conversation at our table in the school cafeteria turned to Jill on that March Monday. I decided to change the subject, and to say something — to say anything — I asked Betsy about her weekend. I knew that she and her family had gone to Maryland to visit her grandmother.

Before she had a chance to reply, Ralph

Nichols strolled over to our table and gave a quick hello, immediately starting up a conversation about baseball with Bud and Gordon. Ralph played second base on the high school team.

Turning to me, Betsy said, "The weekend was okay but not exciting. We took Granny to a Chinese restaurant Saturday night, and the rest of the time was spent sitting around listening to her talk about the past. I'd have enjoyed it more if Gordon had been there. Did you do anything for fun Saturday and Sunday?"

I sucked my breath in, wondering how much to tell her. "Nothing special on Sunday," I murmured. It wasn't that I had anything to hide, and I didn't want to act secretive, but neither did I want her to jump to odd conclusions. "On Charlottesville I — I mean, on Saturday I went to Charlottesville for the day," I added, so flustered I confused the words.

Charlottesville, a small town about seventy-five miles east of Greenview, was the location of the University of Virginia. Like the other seniors, I'd applied for admission to several colleges for the fall term, and the University of Virginia was one.

"Did you go to see if your application has been processed yet?" Betsy asked.

"No. I've already had that good news. A letter came in Saturday's mail saying I've been accepted."

She squealed with excitement, and the boys

halted their baseball discussion long enough to give us questioning looks.

"Christy's going to U.Va.! Isn't that fabulous?" Betsy told them, and the guys congratulated me.

"Gosh, Christy, you're lucky to know for sure," Gordon commented. "I wish I'd hear from Virginia Tech. Sweating it out is grim."

All of us agreed that the waiting for colleges to give us a yes or no was the pits. The boys returned to the subject of sports and Betsy starting asking questions. She had a suspicious glint in her eye.

"You said the letter came Saturday? Then why were you in Charlottesville?" she wanted to know. "Did the letter come before you left home or while you were gone? Saturday wasn't a very good day for a trip. I heard it was raining buckets Saturday morning, and you must have had a miserable ride over the mountains to Charlottesville."

Self-consciousness made blood rush to my forehead and I knew my face was crimson. Betsy's eyebrows crawled halfway to her hairline.

"Christy, you're blushing!" she said, now curious. "What's so mysterious about this jaunt to Charlottesville?"

I wished I'd never said anything about going. Wished, also, that the heat and color would leave my face. All my life I'd been teased about blushing easily.

"*Well?*" Betsy put a lot into that one word. "Did you go with your parents Saturday?"

"No, I —" Still blushing, I let the sentence hang unfinished.

Her expression changed, her eyes widening. "Did you go with a date?" she demanded. "Who is he? What —"

The bell rang, a signal that we had three minutes to reach our classrooms. Betsy was obviously exasperated at the interruption, although I went weak with relief at being able to avoid answering. My knees actually wobbled as I stood up.

"Who was he?" she repeated, her eyes glued to mine.

"Betsy, come on!" Gordon, halfway to the cafeteria door, yelled to her.

"I'll tell you about it later," I managed.

"Coming right now," she answered Gordon, but she tossed another remark to me. "Christy, I'll phone you this afternoon and find out about Saturday. I hope you went with a date. I've been telling you —"

"Betsy, I'm leaving!" Gordon flung the words over his shoulder and she set off after him.

My next class was in the opposite direction from theirs and I was thankful for it. What Betsy said about telling me I ought to date was true. Betsy, Gordon, and Bud, all of them longtime friends of Mike's, were trying to look out for me since I'd been Mike's girl, and they'd urged me to get out more and rebuild my life. To satisfy them, I'd made myself attend a few informal parties that were no more than teen get-togethers. I always insisted that I ride with a couple because I dreaded being alone with any boy except Mike.

Betsy would telephone me after school that day. I didn't doubt it for a minute. It was part interest and part plain curiosity. I made up my mind to plan in advance what I would say. I wasn't going to lie about Saturday, but I didn't want her to think there was anything more than friendship between David Webster and me, because there wasn't.

Nina and I left the last-period study hall together when the dismissal bell rang at three o'clock.

"How did the day go?" I asked her.

"Okay. I don't believe I did too badly on the math quiz because my Ohio school had the same math textbook, and lunch with Kim Clark was a bonus. Thanks for introducing me to her, Christy."

"The first day of anything is supposed to be the hardest," I said, aware that I was repeating a statement my mother made to me when I dreaded returning to school the day following Mike's funeral. "Now that you've survived the first day, you don't have to worry much about the future."

Nina looked a little pensive. "I'm not *worried* about the future, but it would be nice to wave a magic wand and be completely settled in at Greenview High this very minute. Wishful thinking, huh? Christy, why don't you come home with me this afternoon?

My mother is at work and it will be fun to talk and find out about each other."

The trace of wistfulness in her voice let me know that in spite of her outward assurance, she dreaded the inevitable loneliness that goes with being new. During my first weeks in Virginia, I would have folded up if my mother hadn't been at home when I came in from school. It wasn't that I was afraid to be in the house alone, because I wasn't, but I was aching for companionship.

Nina Farrell wanted and needed the same companionship. On any other day I'd have accepted her invitation, but that particular afternoon it wasn't possible.

"I wish I could come today, but I can't," I told her. "Since my parents aren't around tonight to pick me up, I'll have to take the bus. Usually I could go home with you and phone Dad to stop for me when he leaves work or contact my mother, but both of them are tied up. Give me a raincheck on your invitation, Nina. I'd love to come another day."

"Maybe tomorrow?"

"Tomorrow sounds super. I have to run now or I'll miss the bus."

When she smiled, a dimple appeared in her left cheek.

Two

I got off the school bus and looked up at our house. It was a tall, skinny structure painted white with dark green trim, situated in a grove of trees on the very top of a hill a couple of miles from Greenview. We didn't have neighbors in sight, something that had bothered me at first, but I'd grown to love the quietness and the privacy as well as the breathtaking mountain scenery. The house truly had become home.

Dad bought the house and two acres of land surrounding it when we moved to Virginia, and at that time neither he nor Mama nor I realized local people considered the house a landmark because of its Victorian architecture and especially because of its nine bay windows. A Mr. Toscin, who'd been dead for decades, built the house at the beginning of the twentieth century, we learned, and he designed the nine three-sided bays to provide

17

every room, even the kitchen, with an expansive view of the Blue Ridge Mountains.

"Crazy windows," Mike called them. He liked the windows immensely and admitted he'd been fascinated by them since he was a little boy. The first time he came to the house, which was some weeks after we were living there, he commented that he had always wondered how it would be to go inside and look through the bays to the outside. A picture in a three-way frame, he described it. Mike adored the mountains, and that first day he stood in the kitchen and gazed out at the awesome landscape, as if he were in a museum seeing a classic painting.

Some of my happiest and saddest thinking was done when I was sitting on the seat beside the bay window in my second-floor bedroom. My room faced the front of the house, and I could see the highway at the bottom of the hill, while beyond the road, a broad valley stretched for several miles. In the distance, five separate ranges of mountains were visible, and on a clear day, the nearest range was a deep, smoky blue while each successive row of mountains was paler until the final one was a misty line against the far horizon. At night, if I turned on my side in bed and faced the bay window and if there was even a trace of light in the sky, the Blue Ridge would be a black, rolling silhouette.

A lane wound up our hill from the highway, the lane circling the house, and in the backyard the terrain sloped in a gradual decline down to a flat area where my mother had had a flower-and-vegetable garden the previous year. Across the footpath from the garden site there was an outcropping of big rocks, one rock smooth enough to serve as a seat, and to Mike and me, that stone had been a special place.

He and I had sat there many, many evenings in the spring, summer, and fall, holding hands and counting the stars, talking and kissing in the fragrant darkness, while the leaves whispered to the tree branches around us. There had never been enough time for all the things we longed to tell each other, just as there was never enough time for as many kisses as we wanted. And now I was alone.

A dab of bright yellow on the ground caught my attention as I started to climb the hill to the house, and a similar bit of yellow showed beneath a big oak tree near the front porch. I caught my breath. The crocuses were beginning to bloom — the first sign of spring. Looking across the yard, with its wintry, brown stubble of grass and starkly bare trees, I found myself thinking that if Mike had been with me he'd probably have exclaimed, "Hey — know what? Flowers! We must have made it through the winter!" Both of us would have laughed.

Real spring probably wouldn't come to our mountain area of Virginia for several weeks. I remembered that the previous year we'd had snow in April, but seeing the flowers gave me a good feeling. The crocuses hadn't been showing color when I left for school that Monday morning, and they would probably close their petals when the sun went down, but if Tuesday was a fair day, they'd reopen again.

After the crocuses, jonquils would bloom and the forsythia bushes with their long, graceful fronds and tiny yellow flowers would resemble golden fountains. By the time the tulips and hyacinths were at their peak, a green fuzz would be showing on the trees, the promise of leaves-to-be. No more frigid air for months. No more winter coats and boots. No more patches of ice on the roads. I couldn't wait.

Without Mama to give me a cheery hello, the house seemed uncommonly quiet that afternoon. I hung my coat in the hall closet, dropped my schoolbooks on the kitchen table and looked for a snack. A few brownies left from Saturday night were in a tin cake box on the kitchen counter; I selected two, poured a Coke, and headed for the den where our phone was. I knew Betsy would call soon. Monday was one of Gordon's afternoons to work at a supermarket, which meant she couldn't be with him. I intended to sip and munch while we chatted.

Instead of phoning, she arrived in person. I was trying to decide how to describe my trip to Charlottesville to her when an automobile engine sounded on our hill. As she drove into the yard, I went to the door to meet her.

"My mother wasn't using her car this afternoon, so here I am," she said. "Mmmmm, brownies. I hope the one you're eating isn't the only brownie you have." We wandered back into the kitchen.

"Help yourself." I gestured to the tin box. "Orange juice, Coke, or milk?"

She wanted juice, and while I was putting ice cubes into a glass for her, she said, "Okay, Christy. I'm all ears. I want to know everything about Saturday and I do mean everything."

"You're making a big deal out of nothing." I giggled nervously.

"No, I'm not. Please don't make me pick it out of you. Aren't we good enough friends for you to tell me about it?"

We were. I didn't deny that and I owed her the truth. Betsy had been more than thoughtful of me, especially since Mike's death, and she had tried to help me adjust to being without him. She told me often I ought to start dating, and I'd put her off with many excuses, so I knew why she was eager to hear about the Saturday trip.

"I went to Charlottesville for the day with David Webster," I said. "You don't know him, and there's nothing between us. Honest. He's just a friend."

"David Webster." She repeated the name. "Why don't I know him? Does he go to Greenview High? I thought I knew the names of all the juniors and seniors at school. You're dating a freshman or a soph?"

She sat down at the kitchen table and tasted a brownie. I took a chair opposite her, facing the window.

"David is from Roanoke." I mentioned a Virginia city ninety miles from Greenview.

"How did you meet him, Christy?"

"He works at Greenview Memorial Hospital and I met him when Mike was a patient there in January after the accident. Mike knew him, too. And liked him."

I added that last sentence as if to assure her David was an okay person if Mike had liked him. My throat felt dry and I swallowed some Coke.

"Well, go on," she persisted. "Don't make me ask. If he's working at the hospital, is he a doctor or what?"

"I suppose he's an 'or what' and he'd laugh if he heard anybody say that. He's not a doctor *yet*, but he's going to start med school at the University of Virginia in the fall, and on Saturday he had the day off from the hospital and wanted to go to Charlottesville to see about a dorm room and to make arrangements about his classes and to be sure all his records arrived from Virginia Tech. He finished Tech last summer — finished a year and a half ahead of schedule by going to summer school two full summers in the hope of starting med school early. But it seems the current classes are full, so he's working here at the local hospital for the time being."

I spoke so fast I was breathless, and I saw the surprise on Betsy's face.

"What does he do at the hospital?" she asked.

"Most days he works a double shift because he's saving as much money as he can to help with his med-school expenses, so he likes the extra hours. Part of the time he's in the lab, which he's qualified to do since he had a double major in chemistry and biology at Virginia Tech. The rest of the time he's either working in the Emergency Room or lifting helpless patients or, as he puts it, juggling bedpans. He says that's a good way to find out if he truly wants to be a doctor, and he does."

Betsy finished her second brownie and wiped her fingers on a paper napkin. I could guess in advance what she would ask next, and my assumption was correct.

"If he has already finished college, even if he doubled up to do it in a hurry, how old is he, Christy?"

It was the question I dreaded. My cheeks felt hot.

"I'm not sure," I murmured. "The subject hasn't come up when he and I were talking."

"He'd have to be past twenty-one."

I nodded. It had astonished me that a college graduate was interested in inviting a high school senior to go anyplace, even though Lee Carlyle, who was twenty-one, had taken me to a party before Christmas. Lee's situation was different since he was just beginning college despite his age. I'd had a holiday job at the gift shop owned by Lee's father, and at

23

that time Mike and I were on the outs because of a silly quarrel that was my fault. The one date with Lee convinced me I wanted to be Mike's girl again, and I'd turned down Lee's second invitation, hurrying to Mike and apologizing. Mike and I made peace and everything was wonderful for a whole month, wonderful until mid-January when he died.

I don't know why it seemed important to me to explain David's situation to Betsy, but it was. "David doesn't know many people in Greenview," I said. "His job started in December right after he finished his last exams at Tech."

"Where does he live?"

"He has an efficiency apartment on Harrison Street."

"Have you seen the apartment, Christy?"

"Of course not!"

"I only asked. You know him well enough to take a trip with him, so I figured —"

"You figured wrong," I cut in. "He eats most of his meals at the hospital. As for Saturday, he told me he hated to ride to and from Charlottesville by himself."

"I can see that," she said. "I hate going places alone, too. You said you met him when Mike was hurt?"

"David was on duty in the Emergency Room when Mike was brought to the hospital New Year's Eve, but he and I didn't actually talk that night. David wasn't doing medical stuff because he's not trained for that — not yet. But he was writing down names and addresses and taking information on emergency patients and showing ambulance crews where to take stretchers. I saw him while I was waiting with Mama, Dad, and Mike's Uncle Eben to find out how badly Mike was injured, but I didn't pay any attention to David. He had on a long white coat like doctors wear, and I took for granted he was a doctor until he set us straight on that."

"Go on, Christy!"

"There isn't anything else to tell you. It seems everyone working in the hospital who comes in contact with patients must wear a white coat, either a long or a short one, except doctors who wear what they please and nurses who're already in uniform."

"Just how long have you and David been dating? You never even hinted to me that —"

"We *aren't* dating!" I cut in.

"Wasn't going to Charlottesville the same as a date?"

"I — uh —" With a shrug I added, "I guess it was."

"You're blushing again."

"I know," I sighed, touching my face with my hands. "I'd give a million dollars not to blush. Like I told you, there's nothing special between David and me. It makes me feel guilty to talk about him like this."

"Guilty? Why?"

"It's as if — as if I were trying to push Mike out of my life and —"

"Listen, Christy," she interrupted, "Mike *is* out of your life except for memories. I know you can't forget him and won't ever do it and you shouldn't, but you can't spend your life letting those memories keep you from going out and having fun. Sure, you and Mike had something wonderful. I've never known two people who were more perfect for one another. But suppose you had died and Mike was left. Would you want him to be miserable and lonely? Of course you wouldn't. I can see how you might not want to go steady with another fellow from school at the moment, but you need to date and be with boys again. I think it's great that this David Webster has put in an appearance. Mike would want you to be happy. I'm positive of it. So, please keep on seeing David and anybody else who appeals to you. Okay?"

I managed a trembling smile. "Okay." My voice was so low I barely heard myself.

"You think I'm nosy, asking so many questions and giving so much advice, don't you?" she asked.

"I can't blame you. If you were in my shoes and I were in yours, I'd want to know about you."

She drew a deep breath. "Getting back to David Webster, Christy, is he cute looking?"

I transferred a brownie crumb from the table to my paper napkin and drank the last of my Coke before replying. "I don't know that 'cute' is the right term," I said. "He's tall and nice-looking. Light, reddish brown hair and he has beautiful, dark brown eyes."

"How many dates have you had with him? Before Saturday, I mean?"

"We haven't really had dates, although I've seen him a couple of times. One Sunday, when I'd been to see Mike in Intensive Care and was going home, I bumped into David in the corridor. David asked me how Mike was and then said he was on his way to the snack bar for a break, and he asked me to go with him. I did, and later I told Mike about it."

"That was the only time you've seen David until Saturday?"

"No, there was one other time. Do you remember in February when my mother had the flu? She gave me a grocery list and sent me to the supermarket one afternoon after school, and David was in the store, shopping. We talked, nothing earthshaking, just chitchat, and he suggested that we get something to drink and I said yes. I left Mama's car in the supermarket parking lot and we went in his car to Sonny's and —"

"You went to Sonny's with David, when you wouldn't go with Bud?" she gasped.

Her eyes penetrated mine, and the blood rushed back to my face. I wished I hadn't mentioned that episode with David. Sonny's was a soda shop where high school students and almost everyone else in Greenview went to eat and gab with friends. Mike had taken me there so often that the place was filled with memories of him.

What Betsy was referring to was something that had happened on the last day of midterm exams. It was about two weeks after Mike's funeral, and before Bud and Kim began to date. Bud saw me downtown, offered me a ride home, and when he discovered that neither of us had eaten lunch, he suggested we stop for a sandwich. I was seated beside him in his car and as he pulled up to Sonny's, I went to pieces, sobbing wildly. Until then, I had managed to keep my grief in check in public and do my crying about Mike at home in my room, but that day a lot of pent-up emotions surfaced when Bud braked in front of the soda shop. I could not have made myself go into Sonny's without Mike.

Bud was understanding and even gave me his handkerchief to wipe my tears, talking to me gently and saying the same things Betsy said later — that Mike wouldn't have wanted me to be unhappy. I promised Bud I wouldn't boycott Sonny's forever, and some days afterward when I saw David in the grocery store and he invited me to go with him to Sonny's, I decided on the spur of the moment that it would be easier to go into the soda shop the first time with a person I didn't know well, rather than with one of Mike's good friends.

I said all of that to Betsy as she and I sat in the kitchen at my house, not looking at her but focusing my eyes on the mountains that showed through the bay window, the words tumbling from my mouth. She let me finish without interrupting, and when at last I finished, I was aware of her silence.

"Rattling on this way, I guess I sound like I ought to be in kindergarten," I said. "It's just — just that I don't want you to get any big ideas about David and me. Romantic ideas."

"All right, I won't." She flashed a smile. "What did you two do in Charlottesville?"

"I waited in the car. In the rain, no less, while he was in the dean's office. Then we had lunch and in the afternoon we went to Monticello, Thomas Jefferson's home, which is just outside of the town. It was too wet for us to walk around out of doors, but the house was fascinating."

Her smile widened. "You don't have to tell me where Thomas Jefferson lived or that he founded the university," she said. "In this state you don't get out of grade school without knowing about Mr. Jefferson and all the things he did."

"David reminded me that in Charlottesville you don't call him just plain Jefferson. It's Mr. Jefferson and Mr. Jefferson's university."

"Right on," she laughed. "David instructed you well. What did you and he do Saturday night?"

"It was after six when we got back to Greenview and he mentioned dinner, but he'd paid for my lunch and I figured it would throw his budget out of whack if he bought my dinner, too. Mama had made beef stew — she'd said at breakfast she was having that for dinner — so I was sure there would be plenty and I invited David to eat with us.

She'd made brownies. You're eating what's left."

"Christy, you sound absolutely apologetic. Why are you on the defensive about spending the day with David and then inviting him to dinner? If he eats most of the time at the hospital, he probably welcomed a home-cooked meal. Even if you'd given him crackers and water, it's obvious he likes you or he wouldn't have wanted to spend an entire day with you and then mention dinner," Betsy finished.

If I had gone to Charlottesville with Mike, it would have been the most natural thing in the world for me to invite him into my house for dinner. I didn't say that or tell Betsy I still felt guilty about being with any boy but Mike. She knew, of course.

"You only answered half of my question," she said. "After dinner, what did you and David do?"

"He had to report to the hospital for work at eleven Saturday night. Since he would be on duty until seven Sunday morning, he needed to grab a little sleep. I pushed him out before eight."

"Noble of you." She winked at me. "You pushed him out minus a good-night kiss?"

"Honestly, Betsy! You win first prize for speculating!"

"You're blushing again."

I knew it.

"I think David wanted to kiss me good night," I admitted. "I felt he was waiting for me to make the first move, but I — I'm not ready for that. Not yet."

Apparently she realized I was being truthful. "Gosh, Christy, I'm sorry for kidding you," she said. "I didn't mean to upset you, and I have."

"No matter. Maybe it's good that you asked a lot of questions and made me talk about all of it, because I feel better. David knows how much Mike and I meant to each other. He phoned a time or two after Mike died and we talked, but he told me Saturday he realized after each of those conversations that I wasn't actually ready to date. That shows you he's considerate."

"And smart, too. He didn't push you. When will you see him again?"

"What makes you think I'll be seeing him at all?" I put a teasing note in my voice.

"I hope you will!"

We giggled together. A big weight seemed to have been lifted off my back. Keeping a secret from my best friend wasn't a pleasant experience.

"Well, answer," she said. "When will you see him again?"

"Friday."

"And — ? Don't stop there, Christy!"

"David said he'd phone this week and we could make definite plans for a movie or whatever. He doesn't have another night off until Friday, and even if he did, you know how my parents are about dating on a school night."

"Gordon and I just might go to Sonny's Friday night, Christy. If you and David happen to come in, you could introduce him to us."

"You're a sly one," I answered, smiling.

"That's for sure. I mean it when I say I'd like to meet him, though. David must be nice or you wouldn't give him the time of day."

"Don't get irked if we don't show up at Sonny's Friday night, Betsy. I don't know if he'll have other plans."

"Good enough. Oh, no!" She glanced at her watch and jumped to her feet. "It's almost half past five and if I don't get home before dark, heaven only knows how long it will be before Mom lets me use her car again!"

I walked into the yard with her and noticed that the yellow crocuses had folded their petals so securely that not a scrap of color was in evidence. The air was much cooler with the approach of night, and the sun had dropped from view behind the Blue Ridge. Even though traces of pink still showed in the western sky, Betsy had to turn on her automobile headlights. Dusk could swoop down, bringing swift darkness in mountain country.

While I watched, she reached the bottom of the hill and stopped to check traffic before going onto the highway, her rear lights blinking red at me. My mother turned up our lane at the same time, the two of them waving as they passed.

*T*hree

"Here we are," Nina said, as she and I reached her apartment building the next afternoon. "Mom's and my apartment is on the first floor to your left, Christy."

I noticed that Nina didn't mention her father. The two-story building was made of red brick and was set close to the sidewalk with a planter of evergreen shrubs in front. We entered a square foyer with a cross hall leading to the various apartments and a flight of stairs going to the second floor.

Harrison was a short street in the oldest section of Greenview. Some of the houses Nina and I passed after leaving school that Tuesday afternoon had been changed from single-family dwellings into apartments. I wondered if I had walked by David Webster's address without realizing it. He hadn't given me his number, merely saying he'd moved into a studio apartment in an old house on Harrison.

While Nina's building appeared drab from the outside, her living quarters were attractive, with off-white walls and beautiful furniture. She led me through a combination living-dining room and past her mother's room to her bedroom, which had blue drapes and white wicker furniture. All kinds of bottles and jars of cosmetics sat on her vanity; there was a long table, one end serving as a desk with the other end holding a record player and a small TV.

"Christy, aren't you starved when you come home from school?" she asked. "I always am."

She disappeared into the kitchen and returned with a wooden bowl of fruit. Each of us took an orange, and we sat on the floor in her room on fat blue-and-white striped cushions thick enough to be comfortable.

"I like your room," I said. "The entire place is great."

"Thanks, Christy. I like it, too. When we learned about the size of Greenview and how really small it is, Mom and I were scared it might take a long time to find a decent spot to live.

"When did you move?"

"We left Ohio after I was out of school last Wednesday afternoon, drove until dark, and spent the night in West Virginia. Thursday and Friday nights we were at a motel here in Greenview. I was so pooped Friday that Mom didn't make me go to school, so I slept until noon and she notified Mr. Brady I'd enroll Monday. She was tired, too, but she got up and went to work Friday."

My eyes opened wide in amazement. "Do you mean your mother found a job here the instant you arrived?"

"She was transferred here. Didn't I explain that? Oh —" Nina chuckled softly. "I know what you must be thinking. At school yesterday you said your *father* was transferred here and you've probably taken for granted that's what happened to me. My dad isn't involved. He and Mom were divorced when I was eleven and I live with my mother."

I mumbled, "Oh," and for some unknown reason, added, "I'm sorry."

"Don't be embarrassed for mentioning it, Christy. The divorce doesn't bother me anymore. Dad has remarried and lives in California, so I don't see him often."

"And your mother was transferred here?" I repeated the question just to be saying something.

"Right. In Ohio she was secretary to Mr. Winfree, who is with a national trucking firm, and she thinks he's a marvelous boss. When he was promoted and put in charge of a new regional office that is to be built here, he offered Mom a raise to come with him. That's how she and I wound up in Virginia. Mr. Winfree made Mom his executive assistant instead of just being his secretary, which she was before. She's happy with the new title and with having more responsibility and making more money. She deserves it all, too."

"Nina, how on earth did a big trucking firm choose Greenview? This town is awfully small and out of the way."

"I asked my mother that same question. She said Greenview is only eleven miles from a major highway intersection with roads going in all directions, and the district trucking office is to be located in sight of that intersection. She and Mr. Winfree are using a mobile home on the lot for an office now, but the permanent building is under construction; it's supposed to be finished during the summer. As to why Mr. Winfree chose to live here in Greenview" — she gave a shrug — "it seems he grew up in a small town and told Mom he wants to raise his kids in the same way."

I separated my orange into sections and ate one piece. It was delicious. "Do you have any brothers or sisters?" I asked Nina.

"Nope. I'm an only child, and all the stuff about being spoiled is probably a fact."

"Me, too." I laughed with her, although my next comment was serious. "Sometimes I wish my family was huge, but if that were true I doubt if I'd be as close to Mama and Dad as I am now, and I wouldn't want to give up that closeness. My parents are my friends as well as being my mother and father."

"Christy, what's the dating situation at Greenview High?"

I didn't know how to reply. "What do you mean?" I asked, and ate another orange section.

"Do most students go steady? Do you?"

"I only know about juniors and seniors, and I can't speak for all of them. Some don't date at all. Matthew Dunne, the president of the senior class, doesn't date and he's one of the most popular people at school. Of the ones that date, I guess the majority go steady. For a time, anyway. A lot of the so-called big romances don't last long, just one or two weeks."

"Do you go steady?" she asked.

"Not now." My words were muffled and a sudden dryness in my throat made me feel I was on the verge of choking. Nina looked so puzzled that I knew I needed to say more. "I used to go steady," I mumbled.

"Do you mean you and a guy broke up recently and you haven't settled in with another one yet?"

Why shouldn't Nina inquire about me? After all, I was eager to learn about her.

Part of me wanted to say, *I'd rather not discuss dating,* and the other part of me wanted Nina to know what had happened. I blurted out the truth.

"It — uh — wasn't like that." My voice was thick. "Mike died in January and I — I haven't dated much since then."

"Died? Your boyfriend? Oh, Christy, that's terrible! If you'd rather we changed the subject. . . ." She left the sentence hanging.

"Right after it happened, I couldn't talk about him at all," I said. "But I can now. His name is — was — Mike Maxwell, and you'll probably hear him mentioned at school because he has — had — a lot of friends. I can't seem to remember to use past tense about him. Mike was in a wreck New Year's Eve and two weeks later he died from the injuries."

"That's awful, Christy. Were you in the car with him?"

I shook my head. "Another ten minutes and I would have been. He was on his way to my house to pick me up — we were going to a party at Betsy Collins' house. A drunk driver slammed into Mike's car. There were eyewitnesses and all of them said Mike had a green traffic light, but the other man went through a red light and the front end of the man's car hit the driver's side of Mike's. That man wasn't hurt at all." I drew a long breath, steadying myself. "Everybody at school knows about it, so it's just as well for you to know, too. I'm gradually getting over Mike's death. At least, I hope I am."

"You must be getting over it if you can talk about him without bawling."

"I've cried enough tears since January to last a lifetime," I said slowly.

"Nobody could blame you for that. You must be a strong, brave person." Nina stared at me steadily.

"Not as brave as I'd like to be. I can talk about Mike now, though."

"And I thought I'd had it rough when Les and I broke up," she sighed.

"Les?" It was my turn to ask questions.

"Les Tradwicki. He was in the senior class in my school in Ohio and we started going steady last October. It was great. Simply great. Until right after Christmas. That's when we began to squabble. It wasn't big stuff — just little disagreements — but we'd make up and the making up was so much fun I didn't really mind the fusses."

"Is he out of your life now?"

"Would you believe he sent me some flowers on Valentine's Day and then came to my house that night to tell me he thought we should date other people?"

"On Valentine's Day?" I gasped.

"Gross timing, don't you think?" Her tone was sarcastic, but her eyes blinked enough for me to guess she was forcing back tears.

I nodded my agreement. "What was he trying to prove?"

"I suppose the flowers eased his conscience. It's the only reason that makes sense." The blinking stopped and her voice was normal once more. "I can laugh about it now, but it wasn't funny at the time. It hurt like the devil."

"I bet it still hurts, Nina."

"You must be a mind reader. It still hurts in a way, but I'm not going to let it make me sour. Mom told me I'd get over it and be glad of it eventually. She even talked to me like an adult and compared Les' and my breakup to her divorce from Dad, something she hadn't talked much about before. She said she hadn't wanted it at the time but he had, and that now she was glad. It was just a week after Les made his pretty little Valentine's Day speech that Mom came home from work and broke the news about Mr. Winfree's transfer and that he'd asked her to move to Virginia so she could continue working for him. I could see she wanted to accept the offer. Maybe it's a good thing that it happened in a hurry."

Pausing, she ate an orange section. "I didn't want to move," she went on. "Not at first. Mom asked Mr. Winfree if she and I could stay in Ohio until the end of the school term since I'm a senior, but he said he needed her as soon as possible. I've done a lot of rationalizing about all of it since then, Christy. Next September I'll be leaving for college, so my mother will be living alone and she should be where she chooses. Graduating with my class in Ohio wouldn't have been the biggest thrill in the world. I'd have liked to stay there and do it, of course, but —" She gave a mirthless laugh. "There's another angle. I had two and a half weeks of seeing Les holding hands with another girl at school, and that was plenty. Believe me, I was ready to move."

It was easy for me to imagine how hurt Nina had been. Before Mike and I became serious about each other, it was all I could endure to see him walk down the hall at school with Jill Rogers, and I hadn't even known him well at the time.

"What do you do on dates in Greenview?" Nina asked. "There doesn't seem to be much to do here."

"Go to the movies — there's just one theater. Or we sit in Sonny's. That's a soda shop. Everyone turns out for school functions and sports. Baseball, football, basketball, soccer — whatever is in season. I guess the most usual thing is to gather at someone's house for a party. Those parties aren't formal, just several couples getting together. Cokes or Pepsis and snack food are the refreshments and the stereo's always on. Some of the couples dance, some go off into dark corners."

"What about sex?"

"*I'm* not into that," I said.

"Well, I'm not, either." She giggled self-consciously. "I just thought I'd ask."

"Have any fellows from Greenview High asked you for dates?"

"Yes. Everyone is so friendly. Ralph Nichols invited me to go to a movie on Friday night. I said yes because I liked his looks, but I turned down Carl Something-or-Other."

"Carl Browning?" Surprise showed in my tone.

"Browning. That's his last name. He came on awfully strong, Christy. I just don't go for the I'm-so-great-and-aren't-you-lucky-I'm-looking-at-you-twice attitude, which he seemed to have. I lied about already having plans for Saturday, which wasn't true, but I figured I'd find out a little about him before deciding whether or not to date him — if he asks me again."

It required real effort for me to keep my facial expression blank. Carl had been dating Jill Rogers through the fall and I hadn't heard anything about their breaking up. Most of Carl's friends seemed to be boys who had dropped out of school.

"The best-looking guy I've met so far in Greenview is Gordon Sager," Nina said. "Am I hoping for too much if I say I wouldn't turn him down? That is, if he'd given me any encouragement. He said hi when we were introduced at school, and nothing more."

"He and Betsy Collins have been steadies for a long time. They are two of my best friends." I added the last sentence to save her from embarrassing herself with another comment about Gordon.

"Oops! Glad I asked. Christy, please don't tell Gordon or Betsy what I just said."

I assured her I wouldn't.

"Tell me about Ralph Nichols," Nina said. "And about Carl."

"Ralph's nice. He's quiet and has a good sense of humor, and he's very, very gung-ho about baseball — about all sports, but baseball in particular. His father was the doctor who took care of Mike in the hospital."

"What about Carl?"

"I don't know Carl well." The comment was true, although I was hedging. "He — uh

— is a little on the rough side from what I hear."

"That's exactly what I thought. It's why I didn't say yes to him. He acted too macho for me, as if he thought he was God's gift to all the females in the world."

Not knowing what to say, I settled for a small laugh. Nina ate the last of her orange and licked juice from her thumb and forefinger before going into the bathroom to wash her hands.

"I'm happy to have a chance to go out this weekend," she said when she returned to the bedroom and plumped her cushion before sitting down. "Being new, I've been trying to tell myself it might be a long time after we moved before I'd have a date or make friends with a girl, and I feel lucky that you've been so great to me, Christy. Mom felt she was in a rut in Ohio and when I look back, perhaps I was, too, even though I didn't realize it. This move may be wonderful for both of us."

The conversation went to less personal topics after that. We chatted about clothes and school. When dating was mentioned again, she wanted to know which students among my special friends went steady other than Betsy and Gordon, and she nodded as I mentioned Kim and Bud.

Five o'clock arrived quickly. Dad stopped for me on his way home from the office.

Four

The weekend didn't turn out the way I expected. Nothing weird happened, although there were a lot of little, unrelated incidents that reminded me of a string of unmatched beads, and I did something on Sunday that I'd never have believed I could bring myself to do.

David phoned Thursday night, calling from one of the pay phones in the hospital snack bar during his evening break. It was just a little before nine o'clock and I was in my room studying. Crossing the upstairs hall, I talked to him on the extension in Mama and Dad's bedroom.

"Remember me?" he said with a smile in his voice. "The name's Webster."

"As in dictionary?" I teased.

"He's Noah. I'm David. How've you been, Christy?"

"Fine. And you?"

"So busy I need a breather. I'm not sure I can keep up this double-shift routine six days a week indefinitely. Our date for to-morrow night is still on, isn't it?"

"I'm counting on it, David."

"So am I. Darn a town with just one movie house. The picture playing tomorrow doesn't look promising, so what about forgetting the movie and going to the Italian restaurant for dinner? After we eat, we can decide what to do next."

I said I'd like that, and when we hung up, I continued to sit in a low rocking chair in my parents' room for a few minutes, staring at the phone, with my hands clasped tightly in my lap. The Italian restaurant was new. I'd only eaten there once back in December shortly after it opened. I'd been with Mike, Betsy, and Gordon at the time.

With a gigantic effort, I willed myself not to dwell on that December evening, although it seemed everywhere I turned some incident or remark made me think of Mike. Going out for Italian food would be another one. But the only way to avoid those heart-stabbing memories was to become a hermit and stay apart from everything and everybody and every activity in Greenview.

I certainly didn't want that.

When I came in from school Friday after-noon Mama, who had just shampooed her hair and was ready to blow it dry, asked me to do an errand in town.

"This morning I bought groceries but didn't write a list in advance and forgot to get milk," she said. "Do you mind making a run to the supermarket?"

I was always excited at the opportunity to drive the car, and I hummed along with the car radio on the short trip into Greenview. It was another glorious spring day with a rich blue sky and sunshine so warm I hardly needed a jacket. Crocuses, some yellow like ours, others white or in various shades of lavender, bloomed in many of the yards I passed. The lawns had a fresh look instead of the wintry brown of the last several months.

Friday-afternoon business appeared brisk at the supermarket. As I turned into the crowded parking lot, Mike's mother was leaving the store, and a knot formed instantly in my chest. I'd only seen her twice since the funeral, and I hoped if she noticed me we could exchange hellos without stopping to talk. I didn't want to risk getting upset if she mentioned Mike.

I wasn't that lucky. She called, "Christy!" and came in my direction. There was no way to pretend I hadn't seen or heard her without deliberately being rude.

She was a small woman with dark hair like Mike's although the resemblance between them stopped with that. Her face was round, while Mike's was triangular, and her hazel eyes were different from the blue eyes of the Maxwell men. Mike's father, his two older brothers who lived out of the state, and his Uncle Eb Maxwell had the same intense blue eyes Mike had.

I got out of the car, and Mrs. Maxwell and I stood near the rear bumper. My face felt as if it had been covered with plastic film.

"Christy, I've been meaning to get in touch with you," she said. "I know you'll be inter-etsed to hear that Mike had a letter this week from Virginia Polytechnic Institute and State University saying he'd been accepted for the fall. Neither his father nor I thought to withdraw his application after his death. And the college people in Blacksburg must not have known he died."

I marveled that she could speak so calmly. Her voice hadn't quivered once. Her eyes were on me and she was waiting for me to reply.

"That's where he wanted to go," I managed, hoping I sounded as natural as she did and knowing I didn't. "Mike told me several times that Virginia Tech was his first choice."

"I knew he felt that way. What are your plans? Have you heard about any of your college applications?"

"I'll be at the University of Virginia."

"That's very nice.' She gave a faint smile and shifted her brown paper bag of groceries from one arm to another.

At that moment I was sure she was as anxious to get away from me as I was from her. It wasn't anything she said or did — just an instinctive feeling. Being together was a painful experience for both of us; her calm voice was an indication of good self-control, not a lack of caring that Mike was gone.

"I bought ice cream a few minutes ago," she said with a glance at her groceries, "and I'd better get home to put it in the freezer before it melts. Good to see you, Christy."

She whirled around, hurrying toward her car that was parked several spaces away from where she and I stood.

Entering the supermarket, I was a robot, doing everything automatically. I went to the dairy section at the rear of the store, picked up a half-gallon of milk, and carried it to the checkout counter, gave money to the cashier and received change, trudged to the car, and slid under the steering wheel.

It wasn't until I was driving up our hill to the house with nine bay windows that I realized I wasn't crying. Seeing Mike's mother had been an emotional experience and there was an ache inside me because of it, but I hadn't broken down, not when I'd been with Mrs. Maxwell nor later, in the automobile alone. I had been able to talk to her about Mike, even saying his name aloud. Mike would have been proud of me.

At home, Mama gave me an anxious look, which let me know I wasn't as outwardly calm as I hoped to be.

"I bumped into Mike's mother," I blurted out as I set the milk on a shelf in the refrigerator. "She told me Mike has been accepted at Virginia Tech. It's where he wanted to go because he wanted to study mechanical engineering. Ironic that he'll never know, isn't it?"

"Yes, it is," she said softly. "Christy, do you have any idea what type of courses you'd like? That is, after your freshman year. I suppose most freshmen take similar subjects."

"I'm not positive, but —" I sat down, my eyes on her — "working at the gift shop has been so much fun I'd like a business career that has to do with selling. Marketing, perhaps."

"It's a good field and it involves a lot more than merely selling. You'll study economics and statistics and how to make surveys. Many other topics, too. Of course, you may change your mind after a year or two, but that can be a tentative career for you."

I nodded, and when Dad came home, the three of us talked about it once more. Mike had known what he wanted to study in college, and it gave me a satisfying feeling to know the direction in which I was headed.

A three-quarter moon was rising from behind the mountains on Friday evening as David and I came down the steps from my front porch and walked the twenty feet to to his car. Darkness bought cooler temperatures after the warm afternoon.

"Look at that," he exclaimed softly.

It wasn't necessary to ask what he meant. The moon was a dazzling, fluorescent orange color in the black sky. As we paused to stare at it, I felt his arm go around my waist. The gesture startled me, but I didn't push him away and he didn't pull me closer. Somehow, it seemed right to acknowledge one another's nearness under the breathtaking spectacle of that moon.

The moment passed quickly. He dropped his arm, and as if he and I had received simultaneous orders to continue walking, we went to the car.

"Christy, are you positive you like Italian food?" he asked. "I mean, you aren't just being polite since I suggested it, are you? We can eat somewhere else if you'd rather."

"Italian food is one of my favorites," I assured him. "I dote on pizza, especially when it has lots of cheese."

"Amen. My opinion exactly. You're a woman after my own heart." He grinned as he spoke, his teeth very white in the dim car.

La Roma, the restaurant, was in a building that formerly housed a dress shop; hanging baskets of green plants filled what once were display windows. The walls were decorated with pen-and-ink sketches of Rome, Venice, and Naples, and like most Italian restaurants, the tables were covered with red-and-white checked tablecloths. Candles had been stuck into empty wine bottles for centerpieces on each table — the melted wax dripping down the glass in crazily shaped globs.

None of my close friends was in La Roma that Friday, although I saw some kids I knew and nodded to two teachers from Greenview High and to Mrs. Babcock, an elderly lady who'd been one of my favorite customers when I'd worked at Carlyle's Gift Shop during the Christmas holidays. Carl Browning was there with a red-haired guy I didn't recognize, and David spoke to an X-ray technician from the hospital.

The food was delicious and our conversation was casual, mostly about our likes and dislikes. I felt relaxed with David and was glad he didn't rush to leave after we finished our salads and pizza. We lingered at the table until finally he asked what I'd like to do during the remainder of the evening.

My watch showed ten minutes to nine. Earlier, I'd planned to suggest going to Sonny's, but as full of food as we were, a trip to the soda shop would have been ridiculous. We couldn't sit in Sonny's without ordering something, and I didn't even want to sip a Coke, much less eat anything. I had an idea David felt the same way since he'd had more pizza than I did. His introduction to Betsy and my other high school friends would have to be put on hold.

"You choose," I answered, throwing the decision to him.

"Christy, would you think I was corny if I suggested Scrabble? I love that game and haven't had a chance to play it since I came to Greenview. In fact, tonight I put my board in the trunk of the car — just in case you'd agree."

Mike had liked games, too. He and I had often played Scrabble, but I told myself sternly not to think about that.

"Bringing your board wasn't necessary," I said. "We have one, plus a Monopoly game, a chess set, and endless jigsaw puzzles. But no fair using any medical terms in Scrabble."

"I won't. No fair using the names of makeup shades and stuff like that. They're out of my league."

We laughed and I realized I'd laughed more with David during dinner than I had for the past two months.

Mama and Dad were in the den watching a television movie when we reached my house. After speaking to them, David and I spread the Scrabble board on the kitchen table. He won twice before his luck changed, and for the final game, I had all the breaks, drawing the X and the Q and placing both on squares that counted triple. My score zoomed.

"I must not be out of practice after all," I said, smiling.

"I'll take you on at Scrabble again. Real soon, Christy. You say when."

"Not right now, because it's almost midnight. Your work schedule at the hospital will be the deciding factor about when, won't it?"

"That, and your not being allowed to date on school nights."

We pushed our chairs away from the kitchen table. As we stood up, I was aware of his nearness. My parents had said good night to us an hour earlier and had gone upstairs to their room. The house was uncommonly quiet as David and I walked from the kitchen to the front door.

"I wish I didn't have these crazy working hours," he said. "Did I mention talking to Mrs. Taylor, the hospital's personnel manager?"

I shook my head.

"I asked if I could have one free night every weekend and she said she would see what she could do, but she didn't sound overly optimistic. I'm a temporary employee and not many of the regulars want a weekend schedule."

"It would be great for you to be off part of each weekend, David."

He stopped walking and turned to me. "Wouldn't it matter to you?" he asked.

Flustered at his serious tone, I tried to laugh without succeeding very well. "It would be nice for me, too," I managed at last.

"If Mrs. Taylor can arrange schedules and I don't work every weekend night, will you date me, Christy?"

"That sounds like fun." The words came out in a whisper. I felt as shy as I'd been when my family first moved to Virginia. And back then, I'd had trouble even talking to a boy.

One lamp burned on the hall table, casting a muted light around David and me. He put his hand on the knob but didn't open the front door. I looked everywhere except at him, and when he didn't make a move to leave and continued to wait in that one spot, I had to bring my eyes to his. He murmured, "Christy . . ." and his arms went around me.

I knew he was going to kiss me and I wanted him to do it, but I wasn't prepared for the response in my body when his mouth touched mine. I clung to him, my hands clasped at the back of his neck. The kiss went on and on until I broke the embrace. My heart was pounding so hard that my ribs seemed to ache.

"Christy. . . ?"

He barely breathed my name. I didn't know what that one-word question implied.

"You'd better go now," I said unsteadily.

"I'll be back. You can count on it. I'll phone you and we'll make definite plans about getting together again soon."

That time I nodded, not trusting myself to speak. I realized I was smiling.

When the door closed behind him I locked it, turned off the hall lamp, and ran upstairs, taking care not to make any noise. A thin rim of light showed under the door of my parents' room, an indication they were still awake, and I was afraid Mama might call a good night to me or ask something about David. To my relief, neither of those things happened. My emotions were too ragged at the moment for conversation with anyone.

Undressing quickly, I stood in my pajamas in front of the chest of drawers in my room and picked up the framed snapshot of Mike that was my favorite picture of him. It had been taken out of doors the previous summer; he was standing near a tree with his hands in the side pockets of his jeans, his two thumbs resting outside on the blue denim. He was smiling his wonderful smile.

Mike, kissing David wasn't kissing you, I said silently to the picture. *Please don't think I'm being disloyal to you . . . but David is nice and being with him is better than the awful loneliness I've had since you died. He said he plans to ask me for another date and I hope he will. Oh, Mike. . . .*

A sudden gust of wind rattled tree branches in the yard. Returning the picture to its place on the chest of drawers, I crawled into bed and lay on my side facing the window. The moon was no longer red orange the way it had been when David and I had left for the Italian restaurant. Now it was a lopsided circle of pale yellow, giving off enough glow for me to make out the Blue Ridge against the horizon. Forcing myself to turn over, I closed my eyes, but sleep was a long time coming.

$F\underline{ive}$

On Saturdays I usually slept late if nothing special was planned. When I came downstairs the next morning, Dad had driven into town for a haircut and my mother was in the den reading the newspaper. They had finished breakfast hours before.

"How hungry are you?" Mama asked. "Do you want bacon and eggs?"

"Not very hungry. Don't get up. I'll fix myself something."

Going to the kitchen, I put two slices of bread in the toaster and, when they were done, poured a glass of orange juice. I took the food to the den. Mama finished what she was reading and folded the paper, putting it on a table.

"David Webster seems to be a very nice boy — a very nice young *man*," she said. "I should remember not to refer to him as a boy since he's finished college. Apparently he enjoyed being with you or he wouldn't have stayed as long as he did last night."

"We played Scrabble."

She already knew that. I was halfway afraid she might comment on David's age and say he was too old for me, but she didn't. I lifted a slice of toast to my mouth, then returned it to the plate without having a taste.

"Mama, I like David," I blurted out. "He's not Mike, though! Please don't think I feel about him the way I did about Mike!"

"I don't think anything of the sort, Christy. I like David, too, and I'm glad you've been out with him because you're too young to sit at home and grieve for Mike indefinitely. He —"

The telephone rang. Without finishing whatever she was about to say, Mama answered and passed it to me. Betsy was on the line; it was easy to guess what her opening remark would be. My mother went upstairs. She obviously recognized Betsy's voice and knew the conversation might be lengthy.

"Christy, what happened to you and your date last night?" Betsy demanded. "We waited at Sonny's for ages."

"Whoa!" I cut in and forced a laugh. "You sound as if I promised to discover a cure for the common cold or pay off the national debt and I didn't do either."

"You know my curiosity. Did you go out with David last night?"

"Yes, but it didn't work out for us to go to Sonny's. We ate at La Roma and when we left there, neither of us could think of being near food."

"That makes sense. Italian food always fills me up, or maybe I stuff myself because it's so good. Go on and tell me about last night. What did you two do after you ate?"

"Came to my house."

"And — ? Don't stop there!"

I almost gave a vague reply to tease her, knowing that would make her even more curious, but decided against it.

"We played Scrabble," I said.

"Are you kidding? David is through college, isn't he? Why would he settle for that kind of game?"

"People of all ages play Scrabble, Betsy. Play other games, too. Remember how much fun you, Gordon, Mike, and I used to have with Monopoly?"

"I just thought David would be — be different. When am I going to meet him?"

"Soon, I hope." I was eager to talk about something else. "Tell me about your evening. Did you and Gordon stay at Sonny's a long time last night?"

"Until eleven. We had quite a group but not all of them were there the entire time. Bud and Kim came in, and after a while Jill showed up with Carl and a creepy character named Clint Gray. I didn't know him, but later Gordon said Clint was about twenty and had quit school years ago when he was a sophomore. He lives in the county seat, not in Greenview."

"Was he short with red hair?"

"Yes. Do you know him, Christy?"

"No, but he and Carl were eating in La Roma last night. They left a long time before we did."

"Those three didn't sit down with us, just stood and gabbed a few minutes. Jill was in one of her bubbly moods, which I guess was to impress everybody with the fact that she was with two boys, not just one. But you'll never guess who came in as they were leaving."

"Who?" It was my turn to be inquisitive.

"Ralph Nichols and the new girl, Nina Farrell. They sat down with us and stayed an hour. We had a great time. She's awfully nice."

I let my breath out slowly, thankful Nina had had the sense to turn down a date with Carl but not with Ralph, and that Ralph had taken her to the soda shop where she'd see lots of people and, at the same time, be seen. That would help her get acquainted.

"I really like Nina," Betsy went on. "She strikes me as being a little more sophisticated than we are, but I suppose that comes from living in a big city like Cincinnati and going to a city high school. Greenview probably seems small and hokey to her."

"Did Nina say that, Betsy?" I was horrified at the idea.

"No. Just the opposite. She said she liked what she'd seen of this town and she thinks the mountains are beautiful."

Smart Nina, I thought silently. She'd have doomed herself if she had made uncomplimentary cracks about Greenview. I'd moved often enough to realize new people should keep negative comments to themselves. It might be okay for a native to criticize the community, but not someone just moving there.

"Christy, when will you date David again?" Betsy asked.

"I'm not sure. He works an awful lot of hours at the hospital."

"Then he didn't say he'd be in touch?"

"He did say it!" I was on the defensive, afraid her next query would be to ask if he'd kissed me, and I wasn't ready to discuss that. But instead of a question, she made an observation that caught me by surprise.

"Isn't it odd how things turn out?" she commented. "If Mike hadn't been hurt and hadn't been a patient in the hospital, you'd never have met David when you did. Oh, you might have been introduced to him somewhere else later, but you probably wouldn't be dating him now."

I would be with Mike, I thought.

If Mike hadn't been hurt in the accident and hadn't been taken to the hospital, he and I would still be together. That realization must not have hit Betsy.

"What are you doing this afternoon?" she asked. Betsy had a habit of jumping from one subject to another in talking as well as in writing. Her teachers were forever telling her she needed continuity between paragraphs when she turned in a theme or a paper.

"Nothing," I said. "I hope you have something fascinating to suggest."

"Not actually fascinating," she giggled. "But anything is better than staring at a textbook all Saturday afternoon. Gordon won't finish at the supermarket until five. Want to go shopping? I need shampoo and a pair of jeans."

"Okay." Remembering my first solitary week in Virginia, I added, "Let's see if Nina would like to come, too. She's probably chewing her fingernails off from boredom."

"I'll phone her. Unless you hear otherwise, we'll meet in front of Reynard's Department Store at two o'clock."

"Shopping" for Betsy and me meant doing more browsing than buying, and she, Nina, and I had a good time looking at merchandise. Nina bought a blouse for her mother's birthday, which she said was the twenty-seventh of March, and Betsy tried on half a dozen pairs of jeans before she found what she wanted. My only purchase was a bottle of hand lotion.

I'd driven Mama's car into town while the other two girls, who lived near the business district, had walked to Reynard's. When we started home I dropped them off, taking

Betsy first as she wanted time for a bath before Gordon arrived. They were having dinner at her married sister's house.

"Why don't you come home with me?" I asked Nina. "We don't have a fancy meal on Saturday night, but there's always plenty, and we can bring you back to town later."

When she hesitated, I knew she was going to refuse.

"Thanks," she answered, "but Ralph hinted last night that he'd like to come over and I told him it was okay. Please ask me again, Christy."

"I will. My invitation is good for the future."

"I hope so. This isn't a big deal tonight. Ralph and I probably won't go out. He said he wouldn't have transportation. He explained that nobody in the family uses Dr. Nichols' car but Dr. Nichols since he might need it for an emergency call, and his older brother, Bob, is home from college for the weekend. Ralph and Bob take turns with their mother's car when Bob is home, and since Ralph drove it last night, Bob gets it tonight. Ralph lives in walking distance of me and . . ."

She broke the sentence off as if she hadn't meant to talk so much about Ralph Nichols. Probably she was aware, just as I was, that she had a date and I didn't. I decided she was trying not to rub it in.

After Nina and I said good-bye, I drove home slowly, a hundred thoughts swirling in my head. She was lucky to be making friends so soon after she moved. During my early weeks in Virginia, I'd had endless lonely Saturdays when I longed to be going someplace with friends instead of to a movie or a restaurant with my parents. I'd been too shy to push my way into one of the school groups and besides, I already knew that wasn't the smart method for a newcomer to use to go about making friends. Being new meant waiting to be included; it was a hard lesson in patience.

All of that changed once Mike and I were dating, and after his death, it hadn't mattered to me at first where I was or what I did on Saturdays or any other time. But on the March afternoon when Betsy and Nina left the car, I felt differently. The wonderful months of being Mike's girl made my current aloneness more acute than ever. My close friends — even a new friend — had Saturday-night plans.

And I didn't.

A familiar weight pressed hard on my chest, the kind of physical hurt I had whenever I thought about the good times Mike and I had shared. For a wild instant Mike and David were jumbled together in my thoughts. Suddenly, I resented David's double shifts at the hospital almost as much as I resented Mike's death and was furious with myself for those bitter feelings. I didn't have a claim on David Webster. The one kiss at my door Friday night had devastated me, although undoubtedly it meant nothing to him. I was sure he kissed every date good night — or tried to. Hadn't he seemed about to kiss me at my house after we'd gone to Charlottesville? I hadn't given him an opportunity to do it then.

Driving up our lane late Saturday afternoon, I parked in the backyard but made no effort to leave the car when the motor was off. Clouds were gathering, hiding the mountaintops from sight, a contrast to the clear skies and sunshine we'd had during the week. A few birds hopped about, pecking at the hard earth. I saw them without really paying attention to them until they soared into the air and disappeared.

If my weekends were dull, I reflected wryly, there was nobody to blame but myself. I'd turned down Ralph Nichols when he'd asked me for a date several weeks after Mike died, and I'd been almost rude to Betsy when she'd begged me to attend a party Kim and Bud had scheduled for February, although later I reconsidered and went without a date, riding with Betsy and Gordon.

I'd scarcely given the time of day to guys at school who tried to start conversations with me. Betsy'd told me a number of boys had hinted to Gordon that they'd like to date me now that I was no longer Mike's girl, and they were bound to think I was standoffish, maybe even stuck up. I didn't mean to rebuff anyone. It was simply that until very recently, I'd been unable to bear the idea of dating anyone but Mike.

In my soul-searching that Saturday as I sat in the car and watched day change to twilight, I told myself I was thankful not to be boy crazy enough to go out with just any male — whether I liked him or not — simply to be having a date. That, apparently, was Jill Rogers' philosophy and I thought it was stupid.

But when I was with other people, I didn't think about Mike every minute, and the hours with David had opened new horizons. Being with him made me smile again, made me feel alive for the first time since January. I must have been starved for fun and wasn't aware of it until I came out of my shell and rode with David to Charlottesville.

Maybe I was starved for affection, too. I wondered about that. I was part of a loving family, but I also needed another kind of affection. Otherwise, I mused silently, I wouldn't have put so much of myself into David's Friday-night kiss, *would I?* The question jabbed at me. Would —

"Christy!" Mama's voice rang out. She was standing at the back door of the house, a silhouette against the brightly lighted kitchen. "Christy, are you all right?" she called.

"Coming," I answered, and hurried through the dusky shadows.

"Are you all right?" she repeated as I

came into the kitchen, and there were frown lines in her forehead. "I saw the car and when you sat there such a long time, I was worried."

"I'm fine," I insisted, forcing a smile so she would stop worrying.

"Sam Carlyle phoned here in the middle of the afternoon, Christy, and he wants you to get in touch with him. He said he'd be at the gift shop until six and if you miss him, you're to reach him at his house. You have time to call the shop now if you do it quickly."

"Is he offering me a job?" My voice rippled at the idea.

"He didn't say and I didn't ask. Why don't you call him and find out?"

As I raced to the den to phone, my somberness turned into hopeful anticipation. When I'd worked in Carlyle's Gift Shop, Mr. Carlyle had just opened a book department and thought having a high school student working there might boost the sales of paperbacks to other teenagers, which it did. The book department proved so successful he expanded it quickly to include hardcovers. Occasionally I'd helped Mrs. Gibson, who handled china, crystal, and bric-a-brac in the shop, but selling books was my main responsibility and I'd loved it.

During December there were unexpected work hours for me because the school furnace broke and while a new heating system was being installed, Greenview High had to be closed. It seemed great at the time, but caused groans later as classes were resumed on the twenty-sixth of December rather than the customary January second reopening. We had school on Saturdays for a month, a terrible way to start the new year.

I'd notified Mr. Carlyle, when midterm exams were over and the Saturday makeup classes had ended, that I'd like to work for him again and was disappointed that his reply was iffy.

"The gift shop business is always slow this time of year," he'd said. "A post-Christmas slump is normal. I don't need you now, but maybe I will by spring. If I do, I'll let you know."

His *if* was the reason my hand clutched the telephone hard as I called him that March Saturday. Maybe . . . just maybe . . .

"It's Christy Jamison," I said when he answered. I had a mental picture of him, big and bald headed, smiling, sitting in the swivel chair in his cubbyhole office at the rear of the gift shop, with his feet resting on the rim of the wastebasket.

"Thanks for returning my call, Christy," he replied. "Are you interested in a Saturday job?"

"Am I ever!"

"I like your enthusiasm," he chuckled. "Hear me out because I'm not merely talking about one day a week for part of the time. Beginning the first of April, Mrs. Gibson wants three weeks off to visit her daughter in San Francisco, and while she's away I'll need help. Can you come in each afternoon after school in addition to Saturdays when she's out of town? Lee will be on hand to help after his classes, too. Do you feel you can manage that many working hours?"

"Oh, sure! Thank you, Mr. Carlyle!" I smiled into the phone. "I hope this means your post-Christmas slump is over."

"I hope so, too. Sales usually pick up when March comes, and they move forward through graduation gift time and June weddings. Do you feel you'll be able to start work this coming Saturday, a week from today?"

Assuring him I could, I must have floated, my feet barely touching the floor.

Mama was standing by the stove stirring something in a saucepan with a long-handled wooden spoon, and as she glanced toward me, she smiled. "I gather the news is good," she remarked. "It's been a long time since you've looked so happy. Does he want you to work for him again?"

I nodded, beaming at her. Dad, who'd been upstairs taking a nap, came into the kitchen and I repeated everything to him.

"Congratulations, Christy," he said, and put his arm around my shoulders. "You must be a good worker or Sam Carlyle wouldn't want you back. That's a compliment."

It was hard for me to believe I was the same girl who'd fought a King Kong-sized case of the blues just a short time earlier.

Six

Winter returned on Sunday. I came awake slowly on Sunday morning, conscious of a faint rattling sound outside, and I sat up in bed to look out of the window. A hard, sleety rain was falling, the source of the noise, and everything was gray — the sky, the mountains, even the earth was a mottled grayish color. Wispy bits of ice landed on the windowpanes, hung there briefly, and melted. The jonquils, which were standing upright on Saturday, tipped in all directions with their grasslike foliage spraddled and the partially open yellow buds sagging.

My parents had eaten breakfast but were still at the kitchen table drinking coffee and reading the Sunday newspaper when I went downstairs. Mama had on her red housecoat, as I'd known she would. She usually wore it on gloomy mornings.

"What happened to spring?" I mumbled,

not addressing the question to either of them. "This weather is for the birds."

"I doubt that the birds like it any better than you do," Mama said, and laughed.

"Mother Nature is showing us she's the boss." Dad lowered the sports section and glanced at me over the top of the paper. "If it will make you feel better, Christy, I just read the weather report and the rain is supposed to end in the middle of the day."

"What happens then? Snow?" Snow was fine in winter, but not after we'd had a taste of spring.

"Wait and be surprised." Dad winked at me, but I must have looked upset because he added, "The report hinted at a possible fairing off before dark. It's supposed to stay chilly, but the word 'snow' wasn't used."

I toasted a slice of bread, buttered it, and added orange marmalade without paying much attention to the food because I was remembering the snow we'd had in April almost a year earlier. That unexpected snowfall came the day after Mike plowed my mother's garden.

Mama, who was paying to have the plowing done, asked at the Greenview Service Station where she could hire someone for the job, and Mike's Uncle Eb, the station owner, found a man who said he'd come. But the man didn't show up and Mike was sent by his uncle as a substitute, arriving at our house on a sunny afternoon in April with a small tractor attached by a chain to the back of a truck.

Back then, I knew Mike slightly at school and saw him at the service station when we bought gas there, since he worked for his uncle. I longed to know him better, but was sure it would never happen as he and Jill Rogers were going steady. I'd never discussed that at home and Mama didn't know my feelings — at least, I didn't think she did. But she must have guessed I liked Mike. That afternoon she asked me to take him a Coke while he was plowing, insisting that I also carry a can for myself.

Mike hopped down from the tractor when I approached and we chatted — the conversation so easy I lost some of my shyness. He asked if I'd like to ride the tractor with him, and I climbed on, perching in front of him on the bucket seat with his arms on either side of me as he held the steering wheel, my hands on his knees to keep my balance. It was fun and I was devastated that he didn't hang around after the plowing was finished, assuming, correctly as it turned out, that he already had a date with Jill for the evening.

The weather changed drastically the following day and we had snow. I could scarcely believe the miracle was happening when Mike phoned to say he'd like to come to my house. We shoveled the walks before building a snowman, laughing and talking, relishing every moment together. By late afternoon we were completely chilled and I invited him in for cocoa. Another hour passed and my mother asked him to stay for supper.

That was the real beginning of our romance. Before Mike went home that night he said he'd longed to linger with me the previous day after he'd done the plowing. What he did was use the date with Jill to break up with her, telling her honestly he'd found someone else he wanted to date — *me*.

That snowy April afternoon seemed only a week in the past instead of almost a year ago as I stood in the kitchen and stared beyond the African violet plant on the windowsill to the dreary gray landscape. So much had happened to me in the last eleven months that I felt as if I'd lived a lifetime since Mike and I made the snowman.

Mama's voice cut into my reverie. "Christy, what are your plans for today?" she asked.

I took a bite of toast, stalling for time as I forced my thoughts back to the present. To March and the sleet and life without Mike.

"Work on my term paper, I guess," I said. "It's not due until May, but if I'm going to put in a lot of hours at the gift shop the first half of April, I'd better do as much as possible on the term paper now."

She nodded her approval. I wasn't a brain but my grades were high because I tried to work hard. Mama probably understood that work was the best thing for me.

* * *

The newspaper forecast was correct: The rain stopped while we were eating a soup-and-sandwich lunch, and hazy sunshine filtered through the clouds. The cold lingered. I checked the thermometer by our back steps, disappointed at not seeing a quick return of the spring warmth.

There were two phone calls to our house that afternoon; the first one came shortly before three o'clock. Mr. and Mrs. Pearman, friends of my parents, were back in town from three weeks in England. They invited Mama and Dad to their house to see movies of the trip.

"Come with us if you like," Mama said to me. "It's not a party. I'm sure Roland and Martha Pearman will be glad to have you."

It was easy for me to read my mother's thoughts. She wasn't happy at the idea of leaving me at home to work, with no fun scheduled, while she and Dad were having a good time.

"Maybe I'll go somewhere later this afternoon," I murmured vaguely. "To see Betsy or Kim. I might even call Nina Farrell. She's the new girl I told you about."

The tension eased out of my mother's eyes. "I'll leave my car keys on the hall table for you," she said. "Be sure to get in before dark. Dad and I probably will be home between five and six."

I had no intention of going out — unless I was invited. Chances for that were remote on a Sunday, with the afternoon already half gone.

It wasn't that I wanted to stay home alone, because I didn't, but Gordon would be at Betsy's and no doubt Kim and Bud would be together. I didn't want to crash friends' dates. As for Nina, if she'd charmed Ralph Nichols into two dates on two consecutive nights, they might have plans for Sunday afternoon.

After Mama and Dad left, I took a seat at the desk in my room and was pulling cellophane off a new package of three-by-five file cards, ready to tackle the term-paper notes, when the phone rang once more. David was on the line.

"Am I interrupting a Sunday afternoon nap?" he asked.

"No way. I gave up naps when I left kindergarten. Where are you?" I laughed softly just because it was wonderful to hear from him. "I thought you were working today."

"I am. At the moment I'm in the hospital lab, which means this call has to be quick, but I'll have a fifteen-minute break in about half an hour. I thought — hoped — you and I might get together. That is, if you'll come here. Employees can't leave the hospital during short breaks, but we can meet at the snack bar."

I didn't speak. I couldn't. A knot as big as a tangerine seemed to be lodged in my throat, pressing on my windpipe.

"Christy, are you still there?" he asked.

"Y-yes. I — I'd like to see you, but . . ." My voice faded.

"Is something wrong, Christy? You don't sound like yourself. Look" — panic came into his voice — "you don't have a burglar in the house holding a gun or a knife or anything like that, do you?"

"No," I said quickly. "I'm fine. It's just . . ." I took a huge gulp of air and the oxygen must have had a steadying effect. "David, I haven't been to the hospital since — since Mike died, and I don't know if I . . ." I didn't finish.

"Oh, I see. I didn't have any idea —" There was silence. I tried desperately to think of something to say, but my mind was numb. Finally, he added, "I'd better get back to work."

"David, wait!" It was my turn to sound frantic. "I want to see you!" I burst out. "Honest! What time shall I be at the snack bar?"

He waited thirty seconds to answer and it felt like thirty minutes. I seemed to be choking again.

"Are you sure it won't tear you apart to come to the hospital today?" he asked.

"I'm sure." There was fresh conviction in my tone.

He must have realized I meant it because that time he didn't hesitate. "It's five past three now and usually I take my break any time between three-thirty and four," he said. "You can drive from your house here in fifteen minutes or less, can't you? What about meeting me at twenty to four?"

I said, "Okay," and we hung up.

Dashing across the hall to my room to change my jeans and sweater for a blue tweed skirt and a silky blue blouse, I brushed my teeth and my hair and put on pale pink lipstick, noticing in the mirror that my eyes no longer looked lifeless. Halfway down the stairs I remembered something and ran back to my room to spray on cologne.

During the time I was hurrying, I didn't think about anything except getting to the snack bar a few minutes ahead of David, so we could be together for his entire break, but as the hospital building came into view in the distance, a surge of apprehension about going there washed through me. I had driven from home to the hospital many times when Mike was a patient, and now I couldn't help feeling that Mike should have been lying in one of the hospital beds, not buried in a gray coffin in a cemetery across town. I began to wonder desperately if I'd done the right thing to agree to meet David, even though I really wanted to see him. My hands fingered the steering wheel, ready to make a U-turn and head home.

But I didn't do it.

If I left without speaking to David, I would be giving him a signal not to come near me again. He and I might never have another date or even a conversation unless we happened to pass in a public place, and I didn't want to think about that possibility. The last thing in the world I wanted was to lose David Webster's friendship.

With effort, I got a grip on my emotions, knowing I'd have to go inside the hospital eventually and that the first time would be the hardest, just as the first day back at school after Mike's funeral was the hardest and so was my first party without Mike. By meeting David for this first visit to the hospital, at least I would be with someone I knew and liked. It would be easier than entering the building alone.

Greenview Memorial Hospital was a four-story structure made of yellow brick, with a wing at the rear that housed doctors' offices. Like most hospitals, on Sundays the building and grounds were apt to be jammed with visitors. That March Sunday was typical. I was lucky to find a parking space — the last empty one — and I watched other drivers inching up and down the lines of automobiles hoping a car would pull out in front of them and leave a vacancy.

An almost forgotten incident popped into my head, and I thought about the way my father practically went into orbit when Mike and I were first dating because Mike suggested that I come to the service station during his working hours. We could grab a few minutes together if he had a lull between customers, he'd said, but Dad squashed that plan in a hurry. My father informed me flatly that Mike was employed, whether he had any lulls or was busy or not, and I was ordered not to go near the service station unless I was buying gas or unless something was wrong with the car.

Would my father also object to my meeting David during his working hours at the hospital? I wasn't sure. Maybe I was trying to convince myself it was all right to be there. Even though David was at work, I reminded myself that the fifteen-minute break was meant for him to relax and was a legitimate part of his routine. I wasn't coaxing him away from his duties, and he would go to the snack bar whether I was with him or not.

Deciding those doubts were needless, I almost smiled. I was just like my mother, I mused. Dad and I often teased Mama for worrying about what might happen.

The snack bar had the impersonal appearance of all hospitals. It was a rectangular room located off the main lobby and had food and soft-drink vending machines lining one long wall, with an assortment of tables and chairs in the center. I was five minutes early and took a seat at an empty table facing the door, relieved that none of the nurses and staffers I'd met when Mike was hurt were around. I didn't want to think about Mike or the past.

David scanned the snack bar and grinned in my direction when he came in. He walked so fast his long white coat flapped around his knees.

"Hi," he said. "Thanks for coming." He grinned at me.

"Thanks for inviting me." It was easy to return his smile.

He put coins in one of the vending machines and brought two ice-cream sandwiches to the table, each one made with chocolate cookies and vanilla ice cream. They were softer than they should have been, and, at first, of necessity, we concentrated on eating. With a laugh I remarked that the trick to managing an ice-cream sandwich was to do it quickly before it melted, and he came back with the comment that you needed a long tongue to keep licking around the edges.

"The edges of what?" I asked mischievously. "The sandwich or your mouth?"

"Both."

I laughed once more when he took a paper napkin and wiped a trickle of ice cream off my chin.

"I hate this business of keeping one eye on the clock," he muttered a minute later. "There's a lot of stuff I want to say, but I can't get into it with the time ticking off."

"Stuff like what?" I was as conscious of the time as he was, and his remark intrigued me.

"Stuff like —" He was instantly serious. "Stuff like what did you do last night, Christy? I guess you had a big date with a jazzy guy, didn't you?"

The flip comeback I was about to make died. Something in his eyes as well as his solemn tone stopped me.

"Wrong, David," I said. "I stayed home and worked on my term paper."

"Do you mean that?"

"Of course I mean it."

When I spoke again, I surprised myself with a bold question. "David, would it have mattered to you if I'd actually had what you call 'a big date with a jazzy guy'?"

"Darn right, it would matter!" He gave a self-conscious laugh and looked slightly embarrassed. "I guess I was teed off at the idea of being at work Saturday night while you were having fun with some other joker, but if I'd known you were at home studying, I could have saved myself a bunch of frustrations. What about tonight? If you didn't have a big date last night, have those dating plans been transferred to tonight?"

It gave me a strange sensation, an unfamiliar strength, to realize he sounded jealous. I had never considered myself a flirt, but the smile I gave David at that moment was definitely flirtatious.

"Are you asking if I have a date tonight with a jazzy guy?" I said teasingly.

"With whatever," he grinned.

We were playing word games with one another. I wasn't sure whether he was leading up to something or merely gabbing. I didn't even know positively what he meant by "a jazzy guy."

"This jazzy so-and-so may have seven toes on each foot and a face like a gorilla for all I know," he continued. "Don't describe him if you're dating him tonight, Christy. A plain yes or no will be sufficient."

I stopped teasing. "No date tonight," I answered softly.

His expression changed and the brittleness left his smile. Before he looked at me again, he glanced at the clock suspended over one of the vending machines. My gaze followed his.

"Christy, I only have a couple of minutes left, so we can't drag this out," he said. "I get off at nine tonight and if that's not too late for you, since your folks have all those rules about what you do on school nights, I could come to your house." He was already on his feet, ready to rush back to his duties.

"See you then," I told him. "We'll have an hour, more or less."

He probably didn't hear the "more or less." Without waiting for the elevator, he opened a door marked STAIRS and disappeared.

I'd been home about forty minutes when my parents came in. They were full of the Pearmans' home movies and trip. "I always knew I'd like to see England," Mama said. "Now, I can't wait. What about your afternoon, Christy? You must have gone out, since you've changed clothes."

I didn't lie. But I didn't tell her the full truth, either.

"David Webster is coming over for a little while tonight," I said. "He works until nine and —"

"Tomorrow is a school day," she cut in.

"I told him that and told him he couldn't stay very long. Mama, don't you give me credit for remembering Monday follows Sunday?" My laughter took some of the sting out of the words — at least, I hoped it did. She laughed, too, and patted my arm.

"Yes, I give you credit," she said. "Teen-agers have to be patient with their parents. We spent the first part of your lives telling you what to do and what to eat and how to behave, and it's hard for us to break old habits. Give me another fifty or sixty years and perhaps I'll let you think for yourself."

"Just fifty years. Not one more day, Mama."

When she nodded, both of us laughed. She wasn't just my mother but also my good friend, and I knew I was fortunate. I knew I could trust her and I wanted her to be sure she could trust me, which was why I had to be honest.

"Mama, David phoned this afternoon after you and Dad left and he asked me to meet him at the hospital when he had his break — and I went."

It felt good to say it. I hadn't committed a crime, but I'd been brought up to be truthful, and somehow the half-fib stood between me and my mother. I thought she might protest that I shouldn't have gone to see David during his working hours, but she didn't.

Instead, she asked quietly, "Was this the first time you've been in the hospital since Mike's death?"

I murmured, "Yes." She opened the refrigerator door and began taking out food for dinner, not making a big deal out of what I'd just said. I could have hugged her for acting natural.

"Was it difficult for you to go there, Christy?"

"In a way. I was nervous in advance, but David and I didn't talk seriously. Going into the hospital building for the first time was putting another hurdle behind me, I guess."

"Which do you prefer with the chicken tonight, rice or potatoes?" she inquired, and the discussion about the hospital and Mike and David was over.

David and I opened the Scrabble board on the kitchen table that night, but we only played part of one game, more interested in talking. I told him about the gift shop and my job, and he mentioned that he would be free the coming weekend. My first reaction was to feel sorry I'd have to work all day Saturday if he had time off, but his explanation followed swiftly.

"This will be the first time since I came here in December that I've rated a whole weekend away from the hospital," he said. "Next Saturday is my parents' twenty-fifth wedding anniversary, and they're planning a party to celebrate and want me there. It's not a big blast. Just the family and some good friends, but I'd hate to miss it."

"When will you leave for Roanoke?" I asked.

"I finish work at seven Friday night and don't have to be at work until seven Sunday night, but I don't plan to hit the highway for Roanoke until Saturday morning, unless that jazzy guy you *might* date is going to cut me out of seeing you Friday night."

"So that jazzy guy — whoever he is — is back in the picture, is he?" I asked him, using a teasing voice once more.

"You'll have to answer that one, Christy."

"Suppose I put him on hold for Friday night?"

"You do that. You could even tell him to get lost forever." David's grin was warm.

"Maybe we should give him a name," I suggested. "Mr. Jazz?"

"Why not? If I ever meet him, I'll know what to call him."

"So will I. If you ever meet him, David, tell him to drop over and introduce himself to me. I'd like to know what he looks like. I've never seen anyone with seven toes on each foot and a face like a gorilla."

There had been a time when I wouldn't have believed I could talk that way to a boy, not even to Mike, kidding with silly-serious remarks. It was hard to realize I was once a girl who fumbled with words and blushed horribly if a boy so much as said hello. In fact, the first time I met Mike, when Mama and I were buying gas at his uncle's service station the day after we moved to Virginia, Mike began a conversation with me and I was too shy to give him my name.

As David was leaving, he and I paused at the front door just as we'd done previously, and I felt as if I were watching a movie I'd seen earlier without being sure now of the ending. My parents were upstairs, and in the mellow glow of the lamp on the hall table, David and I were surrounded by silence.

"Christy, if you don't want me to kiss you, you'd better speak up on the double because I plan to do it," he said softly.

I didn't reply with words. My lips curved into a smile as he put his arms around me, and I clasped my hands at the back of his neck, closing my eyes, touching his hair, feeling the nubby fabric of his coat.

My mouth responded to his. As before, I was the one to move first and I pulled away gently, neither of us dropping our arms. He kissed me again and I wanted him to do it. And that time, when I made myself step away from him, I thought he was going to say something, only he didn't, not even a murmured, "Good night," before he went outside. It didn't matter. Those warm kisses were all the good night I needed.

Seven

I saw the headlights of David's car when he started up our drive Friday night. I went to the door to meet him, puzzled that he didn't get out of the automobile at once. But a moment later when he finally walked toward me and I realized what had delayed him, I laughed so hard I was breathless.

He wore a crudely drawn gorilla mask made out of a big sheet of cardboard, which was tied around his head with a strip of surgical gauze. And attached to the top of each shoe was an oversized foot also made of cardboard, each foot with seven toes. They were held onto his shoes with rubber bands.

"You were expecting somebody else, perhaps?" he asked in a voice that imitated Dracula.

The porch light was on, and as he crossed the yard and came up the steps where I was waiting, I laughed again.

"Actually, I expected a Mr. Jazz," I said.

"I am Mr. Jazz. If you doubt it, look at my business card." He reached into the side pocket of his coat and removed a roll of used computer paper, which he flipped out so that it stretched several feet on the porch. At intervals he had printed: MR. JAZZ — MR. JAZZ, over and over in huge block letters with a red pen.

"You seem to have robbed the hospital of a lot of supplies," I commented when I stopped laughing. "Where on earth did you find the gorilla face? I can't believe it was in a supply cabinet in the operating room. A smiling gorilla, no less."

"One of the hospital pharmacists is an amateur artist, and he made the mask for me. Did the feet, too. I didn't give him an explanation, so I guess he thinks I'm nuts. Somebody in the Emergency Room spilled antiseptic on a roll of gauze and tossed the entire thing away; I salvaged enough for my needs. And there is always mutilated computer paper any place there's a computer. Aren't you going to ask about the red nail polish on my fourteen toes?"

"I'm almost afraid to inquire."

"Not blood, alas." He used his Dracula voice again. "Plain red ink."

"A nice touch." I pretended to be serious. "It shows you care about details."

Both of us laughed and went into the house.

"I'll consider removing my disguise," he said. "Come to think of it, I'd better do that anyway. If your folks see me in this getup when it's not Halloween or Mardi Gras, they might not want me on the premises."

As he untied the gauze and slipped the rubber bands and cardboard feet from his shoes, he asked what I'd like to do. I'd hoped he'd put that question to me, and my answer was ready.

"I'd like to go to Sonny's," I told him. "Some of my friends usually get together there on Friday nights, and they're dying to meet you."

The last part came out in a rush. I'd debated in my mind all afternoon whether or not to tell him in advance that friends of mine would be waiting at Sonny's, finally deciding it would be best to warn him rather than to pull a surprise. Betsy had said she and Gordon would save seats for us, and David wasn't stupid. He might think he was being set up if a bunch of people I knew well just "happened" to be there.

When he said, "Do you mean I'm to be Exhibit A for the evening?" I figured he already thought that. But he grinned, rolling his eyes, and I assumed he considered it funny.

"I don't believe you'll be Exhibit A — but if you were, you'd pass and win a blue ribbon," I came back. "It's simply that a few people I know are aware that I've been dating someone who doesn't attend Greenview High and —" I didn't know how to end the sentence.

"They're curious about me?" he finished.

That was true, although I didn't want to admit it. I thought there was a trace of sarcasm in his voice as he phrased the question.

"David, we don't have to go to Sonny's," I said quickly. "What's your suggestion about tonight?"

He looked right into my eyes and answered, "Sonny's."

The remainder of the evening was a disaster. At least, that's how it seemed to me.

It wasn't that there were arguments at Sonny's, because nothing really unpleasant happened and David wasn't rude or impolite, but he had very little to say unless he was asked a direct question. I could sense that he was bored, and I wanted desperately for him to have a good time as well as be attractive and witty. I wanted some of the traits I liked in him to show.

Putting all the blame on my school friends for the strange evening would have been wrong, as at first they tried to include David and me in the conversation. Everyone appeared to be on edge, though, and it wasn't the easy session I had anticipated. After a while I grew so tense my tongue felt as if it were welded to the roof of my mouth. It dawned on me that my friends — even Betsy — were acting the way they would have if a teacher from Greenview High had joined us. They were courteous and, at the same time, definitely cool.

We stayed at Sonny's an hour and a half

and nothing about it was fun, apparently not for the others and, I'm positive, not for David. Certainly not for me. I had the sensation of being trapped in a cage that let me look around but kept me confined. By the time I finally figured out what had gone wrong, the evening was over and it was too late to do anything about it.

Sonny's is divided into two rooms. The front room is considered the prize spot, since the tall backs of the booths offer privacy, while at the same time, people sitting there can see everyone who comes in or goes out. They know instantly who is dating whom.

In the rear, past a broad arch that is made to look like a garden trellis with green plastic vines trailing over it, there is a second room, this one square, with rows of wooden tables. Most of the tables are for eight, although more can crowd in.

Nothing is cozy about the back room. It is big and sprawling, with bright lights. You sit there if you aren't early enough or lucky enough to get a booth, or if you are with a large group.

The soda shop was jammed when David and I arrived, and the noise of voices and laughter reverberated. As we passed the booths he said, "Do you see your friends, Christy?"

"They're probably in the back." I led the way under the trellis.

I began to feel self-conscious. The high school students knew I'd been Mike's girl and

that I hadn't dated since Mike's death except
for the few times with David, so people must
have noticed that I walked into Sonny's with
a stranger. The booths were filled and I murmured hello a dozen times to acquaintances.
Those people didn't know David, but Greenview was so small the residents kept watch on
one another's activities. Being talked about
isn't pleasant.

Once David and I reached the rear room,
Betsy waved from the far corner where she
and Gordon liked to sit if they couldn't get a
booth, and we went in that direction. Bud and
Kim were there, too.

Nobody seemed to know what to say after
I introduced David. Just to end the silence, I
commented on the weather and, finally, Betsy
said, "I hope you like Greenview, David." He
replied that he did, and there was silence at
our table once more.

They knew David worked at the hospital,
and Bud tossed out an awful question. "What
does the hospital do with the arms and legs
that are amputated and organs like lungs
and gallbladders that are removed?" he
asked.

"Bud, for heaven's sake!" Betsy sputtered.
"That's gruesome!"

"I've always wondered about it, especially
the arms and legs." Bud continued to look at
David.

"I really don't know." David's tone was icy.
"I'm not a doctor, just a member of the staff."

I was sure he knew. It was a putdown of

Bud but I couldn't find fault with David for his obvious disgust at Bud's stupid question.

The silence was with us once more, hovering over our group like a black rain cloud. Around us, other people were talking, and every now and then a big burst of laughter would make heads turn, while we were quiet. It was painful, so I tried to think of a subject everyone could get into, but drew a blank.

The situation must have gotten to Kim because she began talking a mile a minute about her term paper and how she thought it would be easier to put notes on paper rather than file cards, which teachers demanded. Term papers were hashed over for ten minutes until there was nothing else to say about them.

I stole a glance at David, who had never appeared more bored. After all, I reminded myself, he was well past writing a high school term paper. No wonder he looked as if he wished he were somewhere else. Anywhere else.

"David, I'd like a lemonade!" I said.

A lump was forming in my throat and I wasn't sure I could swallow, but I hoped my request would break some of the tension. You had to pick up your food and drinks at the soda fountain as Sonny's had no table service. As a rule, when one guy got up to go in that direction, the other boys at the table would tag along even if they weren't buying anything at the moment.

"Anyone want anything?" David asked.

Four voices murmured, "No, thanks." The others had been drinking Cokes when we arrived, and now their paper cups were empty. Bud usually nibbled the entire time he was in Sonny's and I thought surely he would join David, but neither he nor Gordon moved. I could have slapped them.

While David was gone I didn't speak. I couldn't. The lump in my throat had grown until it was a rock.

Matthew Dunne, president of the senior class who also played clarinet in the school band, wandered up to our table, standing rather than sitting, even though Gordon gestured to an empty chair. Matthew was a tall, likable boy with hair so pale it was more white than yellow. The only thing I knew about him — other than that he had fantastic musical talent — was his reputation for being girl-shy. Betsy told me once she'd never heard of his dating, although lots of girls seemed to like him.

When David returned I introduced him to Matthew, and at that moment Jill Rogers' rollicking laughter echoed behind my chair. I shouldn't have had any feeling about her one way or the other, but I did. She came to our table and sat down, and I froze in her presence just as I used to do when Mike was alive and she made a point of flirting with him.

Jill had never looked more beautiful, her hair shining and her body packed into tight jeans and a snug, aqua blue sweater. She was with Carl Browning and again I made introductions, only that time it was different. She flashed her biggest smile at David and concentrated on chatting with him, ignoring everyone else, and the awful part was that David seemed to enjoy it. He came to life, grinned at every word she said, talking to her as if he'd known her for ages.

Betsy attempted to start a conversation that would include everyone at the table and got nowhere. Kim and Bud simply sat, and so did I. Matthew Dunne disappeared, and Jill acted as if she had David on top of a mountain. I was angry with him, plus I was hurt that he hadn't shown his real personality until *she* came in.

Carl did a slow burn. After about fifteen minutes he got to his feet, circled the table, and stopped behind Jill. "Ready to go?" he asked her. He sounded hoarse; his voice had been normal earlier.

"Oh, not really." She looked up at Carl and promptly turned her attention back to David.

But Carl wasn't buying that.

"Come on!" he snapped, and when she didn't budge, he put his hands under her arms and pulled her to her feet.

"What do you think you're doing, Carl?" She whirled around, facing him. "If I wanted to get up I'd do it. I don't like being yanked!"

If Carl hadn't smiled and answered calmly, I don't know what might have happened, but the smile took some of the acid from his words. "The girl who comes with me leaves with me," he told her. "And I'm going."

Jill hesitated, then said, "Okay, Carl," but she poured another of her smiles over David. "Wonderful to meet you, David," she purred. "I hope I'll see you again soon. Real soon."

"Sure," he came back, and I noticed he beamed at her.

His eyes followed Jill until she was out of the square room. Once she was gone, his face became expressionless once more. The walls closed in on me. I couldn't sit in Sonny's and watch David's boredom return. I just couldn't.

"Maybe we should be going, too," I suggested, and hopped up. "See you later."

I couldn't wait to get out of the soda shop, and by the time David said his good-byes, I'd already reached the trellis, my smile as plastic as the trailing green vine. Behind me, I heard David's, "Hey, wait a sec," and I slowed but didn't stop. He took long steps to catch up and walk beside me, while I marched through the front room without turning my head to look at him or anyone else.

Outside, the night air was cold and it had a steadying effect, making me realize my behavior probably was as questionable as his. Breathing deeply, I wasn't aware of how fast my heart was thudding until the beats slowed.

"Christy, what gives?" David asked. "You act mad. Did I do something wrong?"

"Of course not. I felt it was time to go —"

"Christy Jamison!" a voice said from across the street.

David and I looked in that direction, seeing a man get out of a car and start toward

Sonny's and toward us. He passed under a street lamp and the light showed on his face, letting me recognize Lee Carlyle. Again I made introductions when he joined us.

"Christy, Dad tells me you'll be working at the shop tomorrow," Lee said. "Good stuff."

"I'm looking forward to it," I replied, and explained to David that Lee's father owned the gift shop.

"Is Sonny's crowded tonight?" Lee asked.

"Yes," David and I answered in unison.

"Really crowded, I take it," Lee went on. "It was a dumb question, because the place is usually packed Friday and Saturday nights. Well, I'm hungry so I'll go in and have a burger even if I can't find a seat. Good to meet you, David. See you tomorrow, Christy."

David's car was half a block away and as we walked to it he said, "Is Lee an old boyfriend of yours, Christy?"

"Heavens, no. We've known each other from the shop."

"He's in the gift shop business with his father?"

It surprised me for David to want information about Lee, but I gave a few details. "He's working for his father when he's not in school," I said. "Lee goofed off, as he describes it, after he graduated from Greenview High and instead of going to college then, he spent a couple of years in Kentucky working for his uncle who raises thoroughbred race horses. He told me he got tired of cleaning out stables, so last fall he came home and enrolled in the community college. He hopes to transfer to a university in September."

Talking about Lee got my thoughts away from Jill, and I relaxed slightly. It was a few minutes after ten when we reached my house. I took for granted he'd come inside with me, hoping a game of Scrabble might make both of us unwind so we could talk to each other and erase the unsatisfactory evening. *Maybe,* I mused to myself, *we can share more than two kisses.* I would have liked that.

As usual, our porch light was burning. My parents always lit the front and back entrances when I was out at night. While I realized it was a safety measure since our hill was isolated, Mike used to laugh about what an awkward time he had finding a dark spot to kiss me good-night.

David had driven straight up the hill and braked at the front steps. Without turning off the engine he put the gear into "park."

"I worked part of last night and all today," he said. "Since I want to make an early start for Roanoke in the morning, I'd better head home and grab some sleep now."

The lump in my throat had gone, but it came back. There was so much I wanted to say — to tell him how sorry I was about the disappointing time at the soda shop and that he truly would like my friends once he knew them better. I wanted to plead with him to stay at my house for just a little while and I wanted to ask when I'd see him again.

But the words didn't come. I couldn't express those feelings, not with the car motor running and his hand on the door handle as if he were waiting for me to hurry and get out. There was nothing I could do but step on the ground.

He walked with me the short distance to the porch and up the steps, standing there while I took the house key from my purse. "David, I hope your parents' anniversary celebration goes wonderfully," I managed. My voice had a faraway sound.

"It will," he grinned, and as I fitted my key into the lock and pushed the door open, he leaned forward and kissed my cheek. It was the kind of impersonal kiss he might have given an aunt or an elderly neighbor.

"See you," he said, and was gone.

I was shattered. Standing there, I bit down hard on my lower lip. No kiss at all would have been better than for his mouth to brush my cheek in an empty gesture. He could have stayed half an hour and still had ample time for sleep. I was torn between dismay and hurt. The evening, which started so well with our laughter over his gorilla disguise and fourteen toes, had ended miserably.

Was it my fault?

Was it Jill's fault? I asked myself the questions. Was she so beautiful and so filled with sex appeal that I was a dud in comparison? Was I jealous of her because she'd once been able to charm Mike and now apparently charmed David — and I hadn't?

I didn't know the answers and couldn't bear to think about it.

My parents were in the den with the television on. They must have heard the front door open because Dad said, "Is that you, Christy?" and they came into the hall.

"Where's David?" Mama asked.

"He had to leave early because he's going to Roanoke for the weekend." I spoke so fast I sounded as if I'd been running. "I think I'll say good night, since I have to be at the gift shop tomorrow."

Mama said she'd make sure I was up in time to go to work, and I hurried upstairs, thankful to be by myself in my own room.

My thoughts were a jumble and needed to be sorted out, but I wasn't sure that was possible. For some unknown reason I couldn't look at Mike's picture. I picked it up, returning it quickly to the top of the chest of drawers. Usually if I was upset, gazing at the picture brought me comfort. I would find myself talking to Mike as if we were together, instead of his being dead and my eyes focusing on a photograph, but that night it seemed wrong to bring Mike into the events of the evening.

I tried to go to sleep. Really tried. And couldn't. Mama and Dad came upstairs, walking softly so as not to disturb me since they must have believed I was sleeping, and the door of their room closed with a faint click. After another futile attempt to doze off, I got out of bed without turning on a light, put the extra blanket from my bed around my shoulders, and crossed the room to sit on the seat by the bay window.

Neither the moon nor the stars were showing and the mountains were lost in the darkness. Like most old houses, ours creaked and groaned late at night, sounds that had frightened me at the time we moved there, although I'd become accustomed to the noises. I pulled my knees up to my chin and hugged my ankles, forcing myself to think about the evening at Sonny's.

Starting back at the beginning when David and I arrived at the soda shop, I went over all of it in my mind, trying to remember every remark, pondering over David's silences and the standoffish behavior of my friends, sifting through tidbits of conversation for clues as to what had gone wrong. It was like working a jigsaw puzzle, only instead of having pieces of cardboard or wood to fit together, I had recollections.

And then I knew.

When David and I were alone together, neither of us thought about the fact that he had finished college and I was still in high school. Age wasn't important. I didn't consider myself as mature or as learned as he was, but we'd chatted on the same level during the trip to Charlottesville and when we'd eaten at the Italian restaurant and when I'd met him at the hospital snack bar.

The gap in our ages must have become obvious to him when he found himself at a table with high school students, just as it had made Betsy, Gordon, and the others clam up. David didn't care to hear about term papers any more than he was interested in the daily activities at Greenview High. He had been polite enough to sit there without griping until I was ready to leave.

No wonder he was bored. I guess that was why he perked up so much when Jill came in with her bubbly manners and sparkling smile. My high school friends were more aware of David's being a college graduate than I was and it made them self-conscious — everybody, that is, except Jill. To Jill, he was a new male to conquer. I had a mental picture of myself being plunked down at a table of third graders, listening to them repeat phonics or speculating on whether their lunch boxes had peanut butter and jelly sandwiches or some other kind. After a little while I'd have been bored, too. It must have been similar for David.

Leaning my head against a pane in the bay window, I felt the glass cold to my face. The bad part was that I didn't know what to do about the situation with David. One thing was for sure: I wanted to continue to date him. And I certainly wanted to keep my friendships with my high school classmates.

A chill swept over me, and I realized how long I'd been on the window seat. Getting into bed, I pulled the covers around my body and hoped that as soon as I was warm, I'd sleep. And I did.

E^{ight}

Going to work Saturday morning couldn't have come at a better time, as it took my mind off David and the events of Friday night. Mr. Carlyle and Lee were in the gift shop when Dad dropped me off shortly before nine that morning, and Mrs. Gibson came in soon afterward, all of them making me welcome. I wore my blue tweed skirt, a tailored white blouse, and my most comfortable shoes, having learned from experience that I couldn't afford to have hurting feet when it was necessary to stand most of the day.

"I'm glad you already know the ropes, so I don't have to spend half a day training you, Christy," Mr. Carlyle said. "I'll be in my office if the shop is flooded with customers, so let me know if you need help. Or, you can call on Lee." He gave a low chuckle, adding, "Don't I wish we'd be busy enough for that to happen!"

Sales were slow the first part of the morning. I made a display of cookbooks, remembering how well they'd sold during the Christmas holidays and, smiling to myself, also made a display of diet books. Lee worked in the stockroom and when he brought a pile of new paperbacks out for me to arrange on the proper shelves, he didn't rush away. I knew him well enough to guess he was in the mood to gab, since I didn't have any customers at the moment.

Lee was a lanky guy with a quick smile. It didn't take long for him to say what he was thinking.

"You were right about Sonny's last night," he commented. "It was crowded."

Glancing away from the books, I said, "Did you get your hamburger?"

"Sure did. Say, Christy, who is David Webster? I don't believe I've seen him in Greenview."

I explained that David worked at the hospital, hoping my voice sounded natural, and as I spoke I put the new paperbacks on the rack, dividing them into categories with romances in one spot, mysteries in another, and the physical fitness and exercise books on a different shelf.

"What does he do at the hospital?" Lee persisted.

"Sometimes he's in the lab and sometimes in the Emergency Room. He plans to go to med school in the fall."

I don't know what made me add that last

sentence. I could have hushed after explaining David's duties. Lee didn't reply instantly and I thought he'd finished inquiring about David, but I was mistaken.

"Are you dating him much?" Lee asked.

I carefully averted my face. "I don't know what you mean by 'much,'" I came back. "David and I have — uh — been out a few times."

"Then you aren't going steady with him?"

"No!" My head shot up. Lee had known I was Mike's girl because I'd told him that before Christmas when he'd asked me for a date, and he should have known that, while I was dating again, I wasn't ready for anything serious so soon after Mike's death.

"Did you say David will be in med school in the fall?" he asked.

I nodded, and there was a puzzled expression on Lee's face. "Does that mean he's already graduated from college, Christy?"

"He finished at Virginia Tech in December by rushing through in three years, so he's not as old as everybody seems to think. He'll go to the University of Virginia in September."

I'd made that explanation so often it should have rolled off my tongue, but saying it wasn't easy with Lee staring in my direction. He gave a low whistle.

"The guy must be a brain," he said. "More power to him if he's that smart, but — Hold on, Christy! Something doesn't add up."

"What doesn't add up?"

"Last December you were really ticked off

when my friends thought I was robbing the cradle because I took you to the party at Sandy Rexford's apartment. They kidded you about being with an old man — me — since you were still in high school and called me some crude names for not finding a date my own age. Remember? So what gives now with you dating a guy who has already finished college? David Webster has to be older than I am."

Lee sounded as if he were accusing me, and I didn't know how to answer. My face and neck felt so warm I knew I was blushing.

"I don't choose my friends by their ages," I mumbled.

"You sure must have done an about-face since December, because at the party you were almost in tears. You —"

He didn't finish whatever he was about to say as a couple came into the gift shop and headed straight for the book section. I'd never been happier in my life for an interruption.

Lee returned to the stockroom, while I helped the customers choose books for their nine-year-old grandson who had the mumps. They soon left, and I glanced to the front of the shop to see if Mrs. Gibson needed me. She didn't. She was showing a crystal fruit bowl to a lady but had no other customers waiting, and I let my breath out slowly. I was glad to have time to myself because the conversation with Lee had been disturbing.

Lee had been right about the party. I had

gone there with him only because Mike and I were on the outs at the time. The two guys who hosted the get-together were students at the community college with Lee, and they were having a housewarming to celebrate moving out of their parents' homes and into an apartment.

I would rather have been with Mike that evening, and the knowledge kept me from enjoying myself. The fuss Mike and I had was mostly my fault, as I was annoyed at his giving Jill Rogers a ride home one afternoon. The day after that miserable party I apologized to Mike, and things were fine between us instantly. Lee and I had no more dates after I explained to him that Mike and I were steadies once more.

But there was another reason I'd found the party with Lee's friends an ordeal, and it was the fault of the other guests. All of them were college students and they'd made me feel I was an outsider. The final blow was their teasing Lee about being a cradle robber. Maybe it was all in fun to them, but it ruined the party for me.

Age wasn't actually important, I said to myself, as I made change for another customer in the gift shop. Or, I added wryly in my thoughts, it might not have seemed important if all my friends and I were older.

I'd brought a bag lunch and a thermos of hot tea from home since I only had a half-hour break at midday. In the past, Lee and I had eaten together in the stockroom. That Saturday I was afraid he might want to continue discussing David and I dreaded the idea, but my worries were needless.

He went across the street to a quick-food place and returned with a hot dog for himself, plus the greasiest looking French fries I'd ever seen, upended a packing crate, and used it for a seat. I perched on a corner of the stockroom table and dangled my legs over the side. We talked, discussing nothing personal and eating hurriedly. Several customers arrived before the half hour was over.

During the afternoon Nina Farrell and her mother came into the shop — the first time I'd met Mrs. Farrell, who was a stylish, sophisticated-looking lady. Nina said, "Mom, Christy is the girl who was so good to me my first day of school," which made me glad.

Mrs. Farrell went to the gift section to choose a wedding present for someone she knew in Ohio, and Nina lingered with me since I wasn't busy.

"Did you go to Sonny's last night?" she asked. "Betsy told me at school yesterday that you and David might show up."

"Yes, we went."

"You don't sound as if it was fun, Christy."

I tried to laugh; it came out as a harsh noise. "It wasn't the greatest, but that's too long a story to rehash now," I said. "What about you? I thought you might be at Sonny's last night."

"I had a date, but we took in a movie."

"With Ralph?"

She shook her head. "I doubt if you know this guy, Christy. His name is Chuck Farraday and he doesn't live in Greenview, but his father does. Mr. Farraday has the apartment next door to ours. The Farradays are divorced. Chuck is in college in Richmond and divides the rest of the time between his parents. His mother lives in New York, and he comes here for a lot of weekends with his dad."

"Is he nice?"

"Would I date him if he weren't?" She giggled.

I laughed, too, but I was serious quickly. "Is Ralph out of the picture for you, Nina?" I went on, realizing I was tossing questions at her the way Lee did to me.

"Who knows? By the time Ralph asked me about doing something last night, I'd already accepted a date with Chuck. Anyway, it doesn't matter, because I don't want to date Ralph exclusively. He's nice, but I'm not going to tie myself to one fellow the way I did in Ohio — not anytime soon. You'd like Chuck. He's very cute looking and he's more — well, more knowledgeable than the high school boys I've known."

I had to leave Nina to help a customer, and her mother finished in the shop before I was free again. Nina waved as they left and I wondered if Chuck Farraday was a college freshman or a senior or something in between. Or even in graduate school. Nina wasn't letting the difference in ages bother her. And I knew I was dumb to let it get to me.

Previously, when I'd worked for Mr. Carlyle, Mike had always waited to take me home at the end of the day. I tried not to think about that as I got into my coat. Dad had driven me to town that morning and he was outside at six.

"How did it go?" Dad inquired. "Lots of sales?"

"They came in spurts."

I didn't realize I was tired until I sat down beside him in the car. Even in low-heeled shoes, my feet throbbed from standing on them all day except for the brief lunch break.

"I hope Mama has something good for dinner," I said. "I'm hungry."

"I think the menu is chili. I thought I smelled it cooking, and she was icing a cake when I left home. I doubt if we'll starve."

He smiled when he spoke, and I did, too, finding that I felt better when I relaxed.

Now that it was almost April, the days were longer and the burnished colors of the sunset were splashed across the western sky. Our house came into view, the scenery reflected in the windows, as if the panes were mirrors instead of transparent glass. The sky was coral and the blue mountains were a soft, misty shade. Mike's mountains. . . .

Don't think about Mike, I commanded sternly, wondering how many times I'd given that order to myself since his death.

Nine

Betsy phoned right after lunch Sunday. "Did you see David last night?" she asked.

"He's out of town. I thought you knew that. He went to Roanoke early yesterday morning to spend the weekend with his family."

"If I knew, I forgot. How was your day at the gift shop?"

"Reasonably busy, but it's a good thing I didn't have any plans for last night because I was pooped when I came home."

That was a face-saving lie. I really had been tired, but I would have relished doing something other than sitting in my room working on the rough draft of my term paper.

"What did you and Gordon do last night?" I asked her.

"Went to Sonny's, then went to Kim's house. Christy, is David Webster always as silent as he was Friday night? It was hard to talk to him, and Gordon said the same thing."

My backbone stiffened. "I don't think he was silent," I came back defensively. "All the people at our table in Sonny's Friday night yakked and yakked about Greenview High and —"

"Gordon just drove up," she cut in. "I have to go now. Be seeing you."

Bless Gordon Sager for arriving when he did, I thought, as I returned the phone to its cradle. I didn't want to have to tell Betsy another lie or think up logical reasons for David's silence.

Two hours later Nina telephoned to say she had her mother's car and would like to come over if I was free. I gave her directions, assuring her she couldn't miss the house since it stood like a beacon on top of the hill, its nine bay windows serving as identifying signposts.

She and I went upstairs to my room after she met Dad and Mama, and she spotted the picture on my chest of drawers at once.

"So this is Mike Maxwell," she said, and carried the framed snapshot to the window, holding it in the sunlight for a better look. "He was really handsome, Christy. Everything I've heard about him at school has been complimentary."

"Mike was . . . wonderful." I fought for the right word. *Wonderful* wasn't strong enough, but nothing would have been.

"So wonderful that no other fellow measures up?" Nina asked, as she set the picture on the chest of drawers once more.

"I'm trying hard not to make comparisons," I admitted. I changed the subject. "Has Chuck Farraday left town?"

"He went about thirty minutes before I phoned you."

"Will you see him again, Nina?"

"I hope so. He said he might be back in Greenview this coming weekend, but wasn't positive. I keep telling myself he probably has a girl — or heaps of girls — at his college in Richmond and was just letting me down easy, but I hope he'll come to see his father — and me — real soon. I won't be his slave, though."

"His slave? What do you mean by that?"

"Chuck's father and my mother arranged our first date, Christy, and I was furious with Mom for doing it. I don't like blind dates. Never have. And Mom knew it. I wouldn't have said hello to Chuck, but she begged. And I knew she'd be on the spot if I backed out, since she's been to dinner a couple of nights with Mr. Farraday. The short notice was okay for Chuck's and my first time together, but now that we know each other, he can't breeze into town and expect to ask me for a date at the last minute."

She sat down on the window seat, pulling her legs under her. "This is one gorgeous view," she said, her eyes on the Blue Ridge, and I was aware that she didn't want to say anything else about Chuck. "I never get tired of looking at the mountains. How are you coming with your term paper?"

"I just finished the rough draft this afternoon and feel like I'm out of jail."

"I know that sensation," she sighed.

"You've done yours?"

"Yes and no. Want to hear something wild, Christy? At the high school I attended in Ohio we did term papers first thing in the second semester, not toward the end of the term as you do here, so I've already written one this year and got a *B* on it in February. But when Mom and I moved to Virginia, I hit this area just as the seniors were beginning their term papers. That means I have to write another one, and I'll have done two."

"Didn't you explain about the first one to Miss Callahan?" I asked, mentioning the English teacher she and I had.

"You better believe I did! I told her first thing, but she wasn't buying my not starting a paper from scratch for her." Nina's lips thinned out in exasperation.

"And you have to start over? Note taking and all?"

"Yes. You see, we could choose our subjects in Ohio, while here the subjects are assigned. I really think Miss Callahan believes I didn't write the first one, that I copied a paper I'd borrowed from somebody or stolen or bought or whatever, even though I have all my notes and the outline, plus the rough draft. My English teacher in Ohio wouldn't return the papers for fear we'd let somebody copy them. She just let us see the grades and made us give them back to her."

"Nina, that's a shame! I should think it would make you hate Greenview High."

"I don't hate the *school,* but I'm not crazy about Miss Callahan. It makes me understand why everybody calls her 'Nutty Nadine' behind her back. I started to go to the principal about it, but decided it would be better to do what Miss Callahan asks, because I don't want to tangle with her. If I get on his blacklist, she could stop me from graduating."

I knew what Nina was thinking. If she didn't turn in a satisfactory term paper, she would receive an F in English no matter how good her other grades in that subject were, and the F would keep her from receiving her diploma with the other seniors in June. She would have to attend summer school to retake the semester of English, and while she would graduate in August, she would be mailed a diploma and would miss out on the commencement festivities. Failing to graduate with her class would be a permanent mark on her high school record, and it might cause her to be turned down by the Midwestern college she wanted to attend.

Miss Callahan wasn't what I would have termed a "mean" teacher, but she was strict, as well as opinionated. In Nina's case, ordering the girl to write a second paper seemed cruel to me.

But even a paper couldn't spoil the day for me. Nina was good company. By the time I watched her car drive down to the main road, I felt like I really had a new friend.

Ten

As March became April, the days slipped into each other in what for me was a mishmash of going to school and, after classes, going to work, coming home to eat dinner and do lessons before falling into bed, and then beginning the whole routine again the next day.

It was getting to me. I remembered the old saying about all work and no play making Jack a dull boy. My name wasn't Jack and I wasn't a boy, but a strange kind of fatigue was piling up inside me until I would awaken every morning just as tired as I'd been when I'd gone to bed.

It didn't make sense. Lots of my classmates had after-school jobs, and I reminded myself that Mike had worked at his uncle's service station each afternoon and all day Saturdays. Maybe I wasn't accustomed to it, I told myself. The truth was that filling in for Mrs. Gibson plus going to school had proved to be more exhausting than I'd anticipated, but I refused to go along with my mother's suggestion that I tell Mr. Carlyle I couldn't continue working the weekday afternoons.

Mama and I talked about it the second Saturday night of Mrs. Gibson's vacation. I didn't have a date and my mother and I had been looking at TV. I'd relished the thought of a night without studying, but the television programs were so boring I became restless. Dad fell asleep on the den couch while he watched, and when I went to the kitchen for a Coke, Mama followed.

She took a seat at the kitchen table and began to peel an apple for herself, voicing the idea of my not going to the gift shop every day during the coming week.

"But I promised Mr. Carlyle and he's counting on me," I said, pouring the dark liquid from the red-and-white Coke can into a glass and seeing pale brown bubbles form on top from the carbonation. "You've always told me a promise is sacred, Mama. Besides, I'll only be working school afternoons for one more week. After that, the Saturday job will be a breeze."

"If you didn't have lessons to do at night, this wouldn't be such a strain on you, Christy, but you look tired and I'm worried about your not having any recreation. You haven't been anyplace lately except to school and to work, and that's not normal."

You don't have to tell me, I thought silently.

Aloud, I said, "You worry too much,

Mama," and laughed, hoping my flip tone would hide the fact that I was more hungry for fun than she knew. I hadn't been out at night or seen any of my friends away from school since Nina's Sunday-afternoon visit two weeks earlier.

"Christy," my mother was studiedly casual, "what's the news with David Webster?"

Every nerve in my body tensed. "I — uh — I haven't talked to him recently," I mumbled.

"Did you and he have a fight?"

"No, we didn't." The words shot out like pebbles being dropped on a hard surface.

I stared at the long, red curl of apple peeling that fell off my mother's knife and landed on a paper towel on the table, gazing at it as if I'd been hypnotized and ordered to look in that direction. She didn't ask another question about David, although I was sure she wanted to know what had happened. I wanted to know, too. There was nothing I could say to her. I was hurt at not hearing from him in the two weeks since his trip to Roanoke, and as puzzled about his silence as she was.

The night before that conversation I'd thought about phoning David at the hospital, deciding to go across the corridor to my parents' bedroom and place the call on the extension where they couldn't overhear me, since they were in the den. I had been studying in my room since dinner and I reasoned that if David was too busy to talk at the moment, I could leave my number with the hospital switchboard operator.

Getting up from my desk chair, I was halfway to the door when my courage vanished. My feet felt as if they were encased in chunks of concrete, making it impossible for me to move forward another inch.

If David wanted to get in touch with me, he would do it, wouldn't he? I asked myself that question a dozen times, always coming up with the same answer: *He hasn't done it.*

The terrible truth gnawed at my mind that he wasn't interested in dating me again. Instead of phoning the hospital, I returned to the desk in my bedroom and sat there a long time, with an open textbook in front of my eyes and my thoughts on everything but lessons.

I should have known it was a good-bye when he kissed my cheek instead of my lips. I didn't know what I'd said or done to turn him off, but he was gone from my life. I was sure of it, and the realization was painful.

Maybe I'd have felt better Saturday night, twenty-four hours after I almost phoned him, if I'd talked to Mama about it when she and I faced each other across the kitchen table, but I couldn't bring myself to discuss it.

My hands, lying in my lap, half hidden under the edge of the kitchen table, had become fists, and when I looked down at them I had to will myself to unclench my fingers. Each palm was marked with a semicircle of tiny half-moons from the imprint of my fingernails.

E_leven_

On the following Friday, as Betsy and I left the school cafeteria after lunch, Ralph Nichols fell into step with us, and without leading up to it, he asked if I would like to go to Sonny's with him that night.

I was dumbfounded. Betsy made a gritty, chortling sound, as if she had crumbs caught in her throat, and said she needed a drink of water, practically sprinting down the hall. I knew she wanted to leave Ralph and me alone, as much alone as we could be with students everywhere, some of them heading for class and others, the ones who had the second lunch period, going to eat.

Ralph's invitation surprised me so much that I stammered. "Th-that s-sounds like f-fun."

"Is eight o'clock tonight okay, Christy?" he went on. "I know you've been working at Carlyle's Gift Shop, and if eight is too early, we can make it later in the evening."

"Eight is fine, Ralph." My voice was less trembly.

We reached the staircase and he went up to the third floor to physics lab while I continued straight down the corridor. I don't know why I should have been astounded, but I *was*. I'd scarcely had a conversation with him since he'd asked me out after Mike's death.

Nina no longer mentioned Ralph when she and I chatted, so I assumed she wasn't seeing much of him and that I wouldn't be cutting in on her turf to accept his invitation. Besides, Nina, with her charm and looks and her sincerity, had her choice of dates, and she'd even wowed Matthew Dunne. Matthew, the guy who didn't date, had taken her out twice that I knew about.

It dawned on me that school was an important part of my life, as vital as being at home with my parents. It wasn't just going to classes and learning things, but where I was with friends, where I met people and made plans for recreation. If I hadn't met people like Betsy and Ralph at school, I'd probably never have known them. That went for Mike, also. Even though I would have seen him at the service station, it was at school that we became friends.

There were a lot of reactions to my Friday night date with Ralph, although it actually was nobody's concern except his and mine. Two of the comments about it — the ones from Betsy and from my mother — were to be expected, but the third one was an astonishment since it came from a person outside the school crowd.

Betsy was ecstatic. After school she made a special trip downtown Friday afternoon, coming into the gift shop just to speak to me. I had a customer when she arrived, so she pretended to be looking at books until I joined her.

"Christy, I almost flipped at school today when Ralph asked you for a date right in front of me," she said in a low voice. "It's good stuff. Real good. If you and he get to Sonny's before Gordon and I do tonight, save us seats and we'll do the same for you if we're there first."

I whispered, "Okay," and left her to wait on a customer who was in the gift section.

My mother was just as pleased as Betsy had been. I waited until after dinner that Friday to mention that I was going out with Ralph, and I saw the expression in my mother's eyes, a mixture of instant relief and a hopeful kind of anticipation.

Her smile started small and spread all the way across her face. "Ralph Nichols seems to be a *very* nice boy from what I hear," she commented, and I wondered who had given her the information. She emphasized the *very*.

"Mama, come off it," I said, and laughed. "You look like I've just been crowned Miss America or something. Tonight isn't a big deal."

"It makes my day to see you so happy, Christy. You don't appear as glum as you've been lately."

I didn't feel as glum as I had earlier in the week, although I was still concerned at not hearing from David. Shoving him to the back of my mind, I was determined not to think about him, and I folded the damp dish towel, hanging it on the rack by the sink.

Ralph's and my date was what I suppose could be called a normal evening — whatever the term implies. There weren't any silences at our table at Sonny's, and everyone chatted and laughed the entire time. Kim and Bud were in the back room when Ralph and I walked in, and Betsy came with Gordon a few minutes later. For once, Jill Rogers didn't put in an appearance, but somebody else did: Lee Carlyle.

Lee was with a guy named Sandy Rexford, one of the boys who'd had the party I'd gone to before Christmas. They paused briefly at our table before going to the far side of the room to join a group from the community college. A little later I glanced in that direction and realized Lee was staring at me. He had turned his chair around and was straddling it, leaning his chin on the back, atop his folded arms. I was flustered and wasn't sure why, but I deliberately averted my eyes so I wouldn't be looking at him.

After a while the boys at our table got up to go to the soda fountain for food, leaving Kim, Betsy, and me by ourselves.

"Christy, when did you start dating Ralph?" Kim asked, as soon as the guys were out of sight.

"This isn't the start of anything," I said. "Ralph invited me to come and here I am."

"I'm glad, Christy." Kim gave me one of her gentle smiles.

"Me, too," Betsy chimed in. "By the way, Christy, do you know the guy Nina is with tonight? They were going into the Italian restaurant a little while ago when Gordon and I were coming down Main Street. He looks older than we are." Her eyebrows went up. "About as old as your friend, David Webster."

I explained that Nina's date might have been Chuck Farraday, who was in college in Richmond, but I was spared having to say more, as the boys returned to our table laden down with milk shakes and foil-wrapped hamburgers.

All of us lingered at Sonny's until eleven o'clock, and when Ralph drove me home, I decided it was too late to invite him in.

"This has been fun," I said, and meant it.

"I think so, too, Christy," he answered. "Let's do it again. I'll call you. Okay?"

"Okay." I left the car and he walked with me to my front door. He made no move to kiss me good-night, and I was glad he didn't.

At the gift shop the next day, Lee scarcely let me take my coat off before he said something about my being at Sonny's the previous night.

"I thought you were all tied up with that Webster guy," he went on, a tingle of accusation in his tone. "If I'd realized that setup wasn't serious, I'd have asked you for a date myself."

"I'm not 'tied up,' as you put it, with anyone," I measured the words out and changed the subject. "Lee, please open that box of paperbacks over the corner. We're running low on romance novels; I can restock the shelves before customers come in."

"Will do." His eyes never left my face. "About Ralph Nichols —"

"Didn't you understand what I just said?" I stopped him. "I'm not involved with anybody! Ralph is a friend. Nothing more."

"That's how I'd like it to be with us, Christy. You and me. I like to date but I'm not ready for a big romance."

"Lee," Mr. Carlyle called from his office, "will you check on the number of Chinese lacquered boxes we have up front? They've been better sellers than I anticipated. I'm going to reorder, but don't want to be overstocked."

"I'll do it, Mr. Carlyle," I answered, and hurried away from Lee, glad to break up the conversation.

One of the lacquered boxes was on a display table and four others were out of sight in a cabinet. I stuck my head into Mr. Carlyle's office to tell him, and as I passed through the stockroom I saw Lee's back. He had a crowbar and was opening a big box. If he noticed me, he gave no indication, and I hurried to the front of the shop again.

That was when the brainstorm hit me. Lee wanted a girl to date, somebody other than the girls he'd already taken out, and I was trying to think of a way to tell him things might be awkward between us if we worked together and also dated — and suddenly the idea came to me. *Lee and Nina.* They would be perfect together. Neither wanted to be serious. Nina was more sophisticated than the other seniors at Greenview High. And Lee had a wider outlook than most of the Greenview guys. He could hit it off with Nina beautifully.

In the next minute, reality set in. Neither Nina nor Lee might like the thought of my arranging a blind date without their meeting first. Nina had certainly made it clear she hated blind dates, and as for Lee, I didn't know what kind of girls he truly liked. I'd be caught in the middle of an embarrassing situation if I tried to throw them together and they took instant dislikes to each other.

It's strange how things work out. I kept the Lee-Nina date in the back of my mind all day, but we had such a steady stream of people in the shop that I was too busy to give it much serious thought. Shortly after three there was a lull and Lee stuck his head out of the stockroom door.

"Christy, I finally located those romance novels you wanted," he said. "Ready for me to bring them out?"

"Give me five minutes to make a place," I answered, and hurried to move the travel display. Just as I said, "Okay now, Lee," Kim and Nina came through the gift shop door.

Nina had never looked lovelier, her golden hair curling around her face and her eyes sparkling. She had on a pastel green-and-white plaid skirt with a white shirt and the sleeveless yellow suede vest she'd worn her first day at Greenview High — the pale colors perfect with her fair coloring.

Lee knew Kim and spoke to her as he put the armload of books on the counter. Kim introduced him to Nina, and I almost smiled because I saw the way he looked at her. Instead of rushing back to the stockroom, he lingered in the shop after I said, "Lee, Nina is new in town. She just moved here from Cincinnati a few weeks ago."

Kim wandered to the front of the shop, picking up first one item from a display table and then another. I followed her and she looked at me and winked.

"Do you sense the start of something big?" she asked softly, cutting her eyes toward Lee and Nina, who seemed oblivious to everything but each other.

"I hope so," I whispered. "They could do worse."

"We came to the gift shop because Nina wanted a paperback to read, but right now, curling up with a book doesn't seem to be on her agenda."

"Did she mention Chuck Farraday?" I asked.

Kim shrugged. "The only thing she said was that he hit town last night to talk to his father about transferring to another school next fall and left for Richmond early this morning."

"So she's free tonight . . . mmmmmm."

"Maybe you should use past tense, Christy," Kim giggled, giving Lee and Nina another sideways glance. "I'll bet you he's already asked her for a date."

"That would be nice. Super nice."

"What about your plans for tonight, Christy?"

It was my turn to shrug. "Nothing. I'll probably start copying my term paper. Gosh, I'll be glad to be finished with it!"

"Don't spend a Saturday night doing it. Come to the movies with Bud and me."

I hesitated, wanting to do something but hating to camp on a friend's date.

"Please," Kim added. "You know how Bud feels about you, since he was so close to Mike. I think he'd be pleased, and so would I."

The smile I gave her as I nodded was very warm.

Twelve

As I stepped off the school bus one afternoon the last week of April, I was thinking what a lovely day it was and how thankful I felt that Mrs. Gibson was home from her vacation, which ended my working on weekday afternoons. I noticed how green the grass looked in our yard. Buds showed on the hyacinths, which meant that in a short time the plants would be a mass of blue, pink, and white blooms, their fragrance filling the air. The early tulips were open, the vivid reds making bright splashes in the yard.

In addition to all the signs of spring, I had another reason to feel happy. Nina and Lee were dating, just as I'd hoped they would. At school she told me she was glad she'd been introduced to him, and when I'd worked at the gift shop the previous Saturday, Lee had said, "Hey, Christy, that Nina Farrell is one cute girl."

"I think so, too," I told him, hoping he might add that he planned to take her out, and he did.

That conversation popped into my mind as I walked up our hill with my schoolbooks tucked firmly under one arm, but I stopped, listening. A strange, rumbling noise came from behind the house, and with a jolt I realized a tractor was in the lower part of our backyard plowing where Mama had had her flower-and-vegetable garden the summer before. My stomach muscles tightened involuntarily and a flood of memories surged over me.

"Christy!" My mother came out of the house and paused on the top step. "Christy, I hoped the man would be finished plowing before you came home," she said. She was thinking about Mike, too, remembering just as I was, maybe even seeing him mentally as he swung the tractor up and down the rows. She must have known how desperate those memories made me feel.

"It's all right," I managed thinly. "Who's driving the tractor?"

"A man Eben Maxwell sent. A Mr. Brown. I asked him to come early enough to finish before three o'clock so you wouldn't see him, but he didn't show up until after lunch."

"It's all right, Mama," I repeated, and walked past her into the house, dropping my books on the kitchen table. I wouldn't allow myself to stare at the garden area.

"Christy, don't sit here and relive last

year," she said. "Here are my car keys. Why don't you go to see Betsy or Kim or one of the other girls?"

She was trying to help by giving me an opportunity to get away from the sound and the sight of the tractor, with the accompanying memories. Without hesitating, I took the keys. I'd have done anything to close my ears to the noise.

I didn't have any particular destination as I steered the car toward town. It wasn't one of Gordon's afternoons to work at the supermarket, which meant he and Betsy probably were together, and Bud had fallen into the habit of going home with Kim most afternoons. When I thought of Nina, I smiled, glad she and Lee were becoming a twosome.

Driving slowly, I stopped for a traffic light in town, deciding to go to the public library and instantly recalling that the library closed at noon on Wednesdays. I didn't like the idea of stopping in Sonny's alone, but I might find someone I knew there and —

The thought ended abruptly. My foot touched the brake pedal as I recognized a tall figure striding down the sidewalk. His back was to me, but I knew who he was. David Webster.

I could have driven by and pretended I hadn't seen him, but I didn't. He didn't know I was there until I pulled up beside him. As he glanced at the car that was stopping, I saw the surprise on his face, his mouth curving into a speedy smile.

"Christy!" he said, and came to the curb where I'd stopped with the motor running.

"You're a stranger!" I burst out, and wished I'd said something else, something clever and scintillating instead of using an accusing voice.

He looked ill at ease. I had to give him that. "I've been having transmission trouble with my car and it's being repaired," he said quickly. "I'm on my way to the service station to get it right now. I asked for a few hours off from work and got them."

Was car trouble his reason for ignoring me? I wondered, not daring to inquire. After all, I hadn't heard from him in over three weeks. He would scarcely have been without his car for that long, and even if he had, he could have phoned. *Maybe he simply didn't want to date me. . . .*

My hands gripped the steering wheel hard as I tried to think of something to say. Fortunately, he spoke first.

"How've you been?" he asked.

"Fine, David. And you?"

"Real good."

We sounded like two casual acquaintances who were making polite, unimportant remarks. Suddenly, we were silent. He stood on the curb, his head bent so he could look into the car window with his face on a level with mine. I noticed how brown his eyes were, and I could see the pores in his skin and the way two tiny hairs at the end of his left eyebrow curled while the others were straight.

"How was your parents' anniversary party?" I asked. And some devil in me made me add, "The last time I saw you was when you were going to Roanoke. Quite a while ago."

He appeared embarrassed, as if he realized how long a time that had been. A slight flush turned his forehead pink.

"The party was a big success," he mumbled, and the silence came back.

That time, I broke it.

"David, if you're on the way to get your car, I'll be glad to drop you off," I said.

His "Thanks" came as he opened the automobile door and sat down beside me. Just to be saying something, saying anything to avoid silence, I gave a nervous laugh and remarked that it was the first time in my life I'd ever chauffeured a boy. *I mean, a man,* I corrected myself. "Which service station has your car?"

"Christy, I don't pick up the car for an hour, and you and I need to talk. How about going to Sonny's?" The words came out in a gush.

Need to talk. The phrase startled me. I don't know exactly how I replied to him, but I must have said yes, because I turned the car in the direction of the soda shop.

A cat darted in front of us, forcing me to slam on the brakes to avoid hitting it.

"At least it wasn't black!" I gasped.

"You have good reflexes, Christy. That

kitty lost one of its nine lives, but it was darned lucky."

Very few cars were parked near Sonny's, and I noted with relief that none of them belonged to my school friends. I didn't want to bump into someone who might sit down with us. David and I said nothing as we went inside the deserted soda shop. He led me to a booth.

"What do you want to drink?" he asked, as we sat down.

I didn't want anything, although I said I'd have a lemonade. The lump in my throat was growing by the second.

David was back from the soda fountain quickly. When he didn't speak at once, I stood the tense silence as long as I could before asking the question that gnawed at me.

"David, what did you mean about our 'needing to talk'?" My voice was so low I barely heard myself.

His forehead was pink again, the color disappearing quickly. "I — uh — guess you've wondered why I haven't been in touch with you," he muttered.

Gulping some lemonade, I almost fibbed and claimed I hadn't wondered at all, but the words wouldn't come.

"Yes, I've wondered," I answered, keeping my eyes on the paper cup in front of me. "I was — I was hurt at not hearing from you, if you want the truth."

"Christy, my not calling you was one of the toughest things I've ever done in my life!"

I recoiled as if he had hit me. "Then why —" Raising my head, I met his gaze. "I thought we were friends, David. What have I done to turn you off?"

"Nothing! I swear it! You haven't turned me off!"

I didn't know what to say. It hurt to look at him and I couldn't stop doing it.

"I hope I can make you understand. . . ." He sucked his breath in. "Remember the night we met your school friends here at Sonny's?"

"How could I ever forget that night?"

"It got to me that night that I shouldn't be taking up your time because I don't fit in with that gang. And if you continue to date me, I might come between you and your classmates, Christy. They're good kids and I'd enjoy knowing them better, but they acted stiff around me and I knew that night they weren't at ease. It got to me after a while that it had to be because I'm older and have graduated from college that they couldn't relax around me. They couldn't identify with me, either. I suppose they consider me a senior citizen or something."

"I thought you didn't enjoy yourself with them," I told him. "You didn't act as if you did."

"I was on edge because I could see the situation once we sat down with them. They couldn't figure out why you were dating someone my age, instead of a Greenview High senior."

"David, is that honestly the reason you haven't called me since you came back from Roanoke?"

"It's the truth. I even talked to my dad about it that weekend at home. He said I might be putting you in an awkward position. I thought about it that entire weekend and especially on the ride back here, and I decided it would be best for you if I kept my distance."

He seemed as miserable as I'd felt since our last date. Without thinking about the fact that we were in a public place, I reached out instinctively and put one of my hands over his on the table. He had looked so upset I wanted to make everything right. He didn't pull away. In fact, he turned his hand over so he could grasp mine.

"The age thing has bothered me, too," I admitted. "I thought because you're out of college that you might look down on people still in high school."

"No way. Would I have asked you for the first date if I'd felt like that? I certainly didn't mean to give you that impression — or give it to your friends, either. What really tore me up was that you weren't yourself that night. You were as tense as your friends, and I was afraid all of it was my fault."

"Don't blame yourself, because it was my fault, too. I want us to be friends and — and —" I floundered, hating to remind him my heart hadn't healed completely since Mike's death. "David," I cleared my throat, "I'm not ready for serious dating but I enjoy being

135

with you. I doubt if you realize how much I enjoy it."

"I'm not ready for serious dating, either, Christy. That's one reason I don't want to come between you and your friends. I have four years of med school ahead of me plus a couple more years of interning and residency after that, and it won't leave a lot of room for fun. But I don't intend to become a work freak and do nothing but study. I can truthfully say I like you better than any girl I've met in a long, long time, so can't we be friends? Really good friends."

"I can." I smiled at him.

"Me, too, Christy."

I felt as if a heavy load had rolled off my back. Gently pulling my hand from his, I rested it in my lap, my fingers burning from his touch.

"Hey, I need that hand," he grinned. "You don't want me to hold it?"

"I do like it. . . ." I brought the hand back to the tabletop and felt David's palm cover my fingers once more. I wanted desperately for him to realize that not all my friends would be as ill at ease with him as the group at Sonny's had been that other night. David might be happier with people nearer his own age. . . .

With Lee and Nina?

I was positive of it. After he came to know Lee and Nina, maybe he and I could plan an evening with Kim and Bud or with Betsy and

Gordon, without taking on the entire high school group at one time.

"David, you met Lee Carlyle the other night," I said. "He's dating a girl named Nina Farrell who just moved here from Ohio, and she's a senior at Greenview High just as I am. How would you feel about our double-dating with them? Maybe we can plan something. . . ." My voice trailed off.

"Sure."

"Do you mean it?"

"Cross my heart and hope to die. Know something? I haven't said that phrase since I was in grade school."

We laughed together and he squeezed my hand gently. It was amazing that I could be in the soda shop holding hands with a boy and not feel the least bit self-conscious.

"I don't work this Sunday afternoon, Christy," he went on. "I'm off at three o'clock and don't go back to the grind until eleven that night."

"A picnic! Let's have a picnic! The weather is warm enough and —"

"You're positively sparkling," he interrupted me. "A picnic sounds great. Where is a good spot for it?"

I couldn't bring myself to suggest any of the places Mike and I had picnicked, but I had a suggestion. "Lee has lived here all his life," I said. "He'll know where we can go."

"You check with your friends and if they can't make it Sunday, there's no reason you and I can't have our picnic."

A short time later, when David and I left Sonny's, I was afraid he might want me to drive him to the Greenview Service Station for his car, and I shuddered inwardly at the prospect of stopping there and having Mike's Uncle Eb find me with another boy. But luckily, David's car was at a garage across town. We said hurried good-byes as soon as we reached there.

"See you soon," he told me as he left my car. "I'll phone you soon, and don't forget the picnic. Keep your fingers crossed for sunshine."

"Will do." Smiling, I drove away with one last glance at him in the rearview mirror, aware that I felt very different from the way I had when I'd left home. I'd almost gone to pieces at the sound of a tractor, and I'd driven down our hill just to get away from hurting memories.

I still had those memories, but they weren't as painful as they'd been. Seeing David had made the difference, and now I could look forward to seeing him again. Things were right between us.

A soft breeze came through the open windows of the car. I glanced at the mountains, drinking in the beauty around me, more lighthearted than I'd felt in ages. For the first time, I dared to admit to myself that not seeing David had put a terrible void in my life.

Thirteen

David lay on his back on the grass, with his arms stretched over his head, his eyes closed and his breathing so deep I thought he might have fallen asleep. I was sitting cross-legged beside him, my back resting against an oak tree. Half an hour earlier Nina and Lee had decided to take a walk; they were following a narrow stream that curved and gurgled its way across the meadow.

They had been as enthusiastic about the picnic as David and I had, and Lee knew of an ideal place for us to go Sunday afternoon. "My parents own a small farm a few miles from town," he said, when I approached him. "They plan to build a house there eventually and live in the country, but for right now, it's only woods and pastureland. Dad rents the grazing rights to a dairyman who lives down the road, but the cows are fenced in. They won't bother us."

"And we won't bother them," Nina said with a giggle. "You know, I've never been close to a cow."

"The only building on the premises is what's left of a barn," Lee went on. "It's falling down, but we keep some yard chairs and a barbecue grill there, and the barn is somewhere to wait out a rain."

"Rain won't fall on this picnic," I announced. "I refuse to let it happen."

And it hadn't happened. Sunday was glorious — warm and sunny with a few puffy clouds sliding across the blue sky. David and I rode to Mr. Carlyle's farm with Lee and Nina in Lee's car, the road winding around a small mountain that Lee called "a knob." He finally left the road and drove down a one-lane clearing, stopping beside a cluster of trees in sight of a stream. The dilapidated barn was a few yards to the left, and on the right, the grassy land dipped and rolled to more woods.

Lee brought four canvas chairs from the barn, but we opted to sit on the mossy grass. Charcoal was lit on the grill, the flames shooting up and then dying while the coals slowly became red. Since it was too early to eat, Nina suggested a walk.

"Not me," David replied. "I've been walking up and down the hospital halls for hours and I'll do it again tomorrow. I intend to lie right here and think deep thoughts. Christy, you go for a walk with them if you want."

I shook my head. "I'll think deep thoughts,

too," I murmured, and watched Lee and Nina trudge along the stream bank hand in hand.

At first David and I chatted a little, not saying anything serious. I remarked that one cloud looked like an old lady sweeping, and he said, "Do you like to find pictures in clouds? I haven't done that since I was a kid, but I used to get a bang out of it."

"I did it for hours to amuse myself in the car when I was little," I told him. "Look at the old lady. She's disintegrating, and her broom looks like a rifle now."

"Or a hockey stick."

"Maybe she's a witch. Her head's getting pointed."

We laughed and fell silent again. Birds sang off in the distance. Tree branches were covered with pale green fuzz that would be leaves eventually, those branches moving occasionally when the wind sprang up. I leaned against the oak, the bark rough to my shoulders through the knitted shirt I was wearing with my jeans. David continued to gaze at the sky until I noticed his eyes were drooping, and when his breathing slowed, I was sure he'd dozed off.

"Are you still here, Christy?" he asked unexpectedly some minutes later.

"Right here." I reached out and touched his cheek with my fingertips. "I thought you were dead to the world."

"Nope. Just enjoying the peace and quiet."

"What happened to all those deep thoughts you planned to think?"

"They must have disappeared with the breeze."

He rolled over on his stomach and propped himself up on his elbows, then changed positions once more and sat beside me, facing in the opposite direction, making us inches apart. His eyes had a smoky look; he seemed to be watching me with a strange intentness.

I knew he was going to kiss me. He didn't have to say it, but his gaze went to my lips and I knew — the way a girl always knows. And I wanted that kiss.

"Christy. . . ." Leaning toward me, he brushed his mouth against mine before putting his arms around my shoulders and pulling me gently against his chest. I was breathless when the kisses ended. I didn't realize my eyes had been shut until I opened them. He was opening his eyes at the same moment.

"Hi," he whispered.

"Hi, yourself."

"You have a beautiful mouth, Christy. I like kissing you."

"I like kissing you back." I knew I was smiling. Leaning forward again, he kissed me once more.

The sound of Nina's laughter made us pull apart. Nina and Lee were in the distance, coming toward us and walking along the edge of the stream. I could guess Nina had been kissed, too. Her cheeks were flushed and Lee's arm was around her waist.

"Did you two explorers find the end of the stream?" David asked.

"Of course," Nina came back. "Lee knew all the time that it ended in a pond his father dammed up to make a drinking place for the cows."

"Nina had her first close-up look at a cow," Lee chuckled. "On the other side of the fence, of course. They really took each other in."

"Well, what do you think of cows?" David pretended to be serious.

"Big, beautiful brown eyes, but not much personality. They didn't even moo but they looked at me and I looked at them and then we went our separate ways."

Lee examined the grill. "I think the coals are just right for cooking hamburgers," he said. "Anybody hungry?"

Three voices said "Yes" in unison, and we bustled around getting lunch ready. The boys had brought the meat, rolls, and Cokes. Nina had prepared a huge tossed salad, and, to keep it fresh, she'd wrapped ice cubes in foil and laid them on top of the wooden bowl of greens. I'd made cupcakes, icing some with chocolate and the others with orange frosting, and I'd brought a jar of Mama's home-made cucumber pickles plus some bananas we had on hand.

Laughter and conversation flowed while we ate, although once the food was gone, we were content to sit silently. Talk didn't seem necessary as the sun went down behind the distant mountains and a thin, little moon was visible in the darkening sky. Nina began to hum a popular song with a slow tempo, and the rest of us joined in, going to another tune when the first one was finished. It would have seemed a sacrilege to sing something loud or with a heavy beat; the lilting, melodious songs were just right. David's arm was around me and I leaned against him instead of against the big oak, while Lee lay on the ground with his head in Nina's lap.

None of us wanted to leave, but shortly after ten Lee asked if David had night duty at the hospital.

"Not tonight, thank goodness," David replied. "I go at seven in the morning."

"I have to be home by eleven, so I guess I'll be the one to break this up," Nina sighed. "Mom reminded me that tomorrow is a school day — as if I could forget."

"That goes for me, too," I added.

Lee got to his feet and brushed loose grass from his jeans. "You two make it through one more month and you won't have to worry about school nights for a while," he remarked. "Not until fall, and by then you'll be in college."

It was hard to realize that in just one more month I'd leave high school behind forever.

All of a sudden I was frightened, and it must have showed. David said, "Something wrong, Christy?"

"I don't know." I caught my breath. "I know how to act at high school and what's expected of me, but it will be different at college. I hate to admit it, but I'm scared."

"You'll be okay." David slipped his arm

around my shoulders. "Just be yourself. The people who have problems in college usually are the ones who come on too strong and try to tell everybody else how great they are. I know you'll be fine."

"Me, too?" Nina asked. She smiled, but she was serious.

"Yep, you, too." David grinned at her. Lee nodded.

David had left his car in my backyard, and we stood beside it until Lee and Nina were out of sight. Five minutes to eleven was too late for me to invite a boy in — I knew I'd hear about it later from Mama if I did. Our porch light was on, and David deliberately led me to the shadows.

"Today has been fun," I murmured.

"For me, too, Christy."

He cupped his hands around my face and kissed me. "I don't know whether I'll be free next weekend or not, but I'll let you know. You'd better get in the house now. I could stand here for hours and kiss you, but I'd hate to get on your parents' blacklist of people they don't want on the premises."

I smiled at him. "It'll never happen."

After a final kiss, he walked with me to the circle of light by the front door, standing there until I was safely inside.

Mama and Dad wanted to know about the picnic and I described the setting, mentioning how good the food was and that all her pickles were eaten, adding that we sang a long time. But I said nothing about David's and my kisses. My parents planned to stay up another half hour to see a news special on TV, and I went upstairs.

The crescent moon was visible from my window and the stars had never appeared brighter. I stood in the darkness a little while, looking at the mountains, my lips still burning from David's kisses. Did he feel that same fire? I wish I knew.

For once I didn't pick up Mike's picture and stare at it. Somehow, that would have been wrong under the circumstances, although as I undressed and slid into bed, I was thinking about Mike and found myself telling him about the evening. It was a special kind of communication that had developed between us since his death. I didn't need to say the actual words, but he seemed close to me and, at the same time, very far away.

It was strange, but as I lay there half asleep, Mike and David were mixed up together in my thoughts. They weren't one and the same person, but. . . . Sleep must have caught up with me because thinking took too much effort, and the next day all those vague, hazy thoughts were gone.

Fourteen

The month of May whizzed by so quickly that I felt as if I were riding a roller coaster. On Saturdays I continued to work at the gift shop, and many of my weekday afternoons were spent at school helping with graduation arrangements.

Girls were asked to wear white dresses under their caps and gowns, so Mama and I went shopping. We found a darling white cotton dress made in a tailored style, with a tiny edging of lace around the collar and cuffs.

David and I talked on the phone often, both of us hating the fact that he had so much weekend duty at the hospital, but we managed to see each other whenever possible. We went to the movies one Friday night, and on two successive Sundays, I met him at the hospital snack bar during his afternoon breaks. Mama and Dad relaxed their no-dating-on-school-nights rule by allowing me to invite him to dinner when he had a free evening during the week. I promised them I'd see that he left by ten. And he couldn't have been more cooperative.

"Mama must figure I'm growing up at last," I giggled to David, and saw his answering grin the first time he came over on a school night. He and I were standing in the hall saying our good-byes. "Otherwise," I added, "I'd be in my room studying right now."

"It must be hard on parents to have their kids stop being kids," he said, taking my hand in one of his. He folded his fingers around my palm. "My folks are like that, too. I'm glad we could be together tonight."

"So am I," I said softly.

"I already know I'll have duty the next two weekends. One of the lab technicians has resigned without giving any notice. The hospital doesn't have a replacement for her yet, and another one is out on maternity leave and won't return for three weeks. Also, the Emergency Room has been busier than usual lately. We've had wreck injuries, heart attacks, burns — you name it and we've had the rescue squad ambulances bringing cases in. I know I'm needed and I'm darned lucky to have this job, so I can't make waves about the hours, even though the schedule means cutting down on the time we'd have for fun."

"I know. . ."

I was about to say more but didn't, because

he reached out to trace the outline of my lips with his forefinger, a tender smile on his face, and I waited for the kiss I knew would be coming, then went with him to the porch where we kissed again.

Just because David and I couldn't date often didn't mean I stayed home alone every weekend. Ralph Nichols took me to Sonny's several times, and one Friday night, when Nina had a crowd over, she said she'd asked Matthew Dunne to bring me. She was still seeing a great deal of Lee Carlyle, who was her date that evening.

I realized it was time for me to invite a crowd of school friends to my house, something I hadn't done since Mike's death, although I wasn't quite ready to do it. Maybe I would during the summer, I reminded myself.

"Christy, Matthew seemed pleased when I mentioned you," Nina went on. "I have the feeling he's been dying to date you and is afraid you might turn him down."

"What makes him think that? I don't know him well, but I think he's nice."

"He can't forget that you were Mike's girl and that now you go out a lot with David. Also, Matthew hasn't been dating long and he's still a little uneasy around girls. Christy" — she gave me a pensive smile — "I wish David could come to my party. I phoned him at the hospital and invited him — that was before I spoke to Matthew about stopping for you, of course — but David said he had to work. The picnic you and he had with Lee and me was super. I want us to have another one."

I thanked her for thinking of David. "You don't object to coming with Matthew, do you?" she asked.

"I'm looking forward to it."

Nina's party was great, and as Matthew was driving me home afterward, he asked me to go to the movies with him the following evening. That was enjoyable, too. We bumped into Kim and Bud in the ticket line at the theater, so the four of us sat together.

So I was always busy, and in the hustle of activities I was able to put thoughts of graduation — and college — behind me.

Fifteen

When I came home from work one Saturday afternoon toward the end of May, Mama said Betsy wanted me to telephone her at once.

"Betsy called here twice in the last hour," my mother went on. "I told her you didn't leave the gift shop until six and that your dad would pick you up. Whatever she has on her mind must be important."

Going to the den phone, I dialed Betsy's number, and she barely let me say, "Hello," before she burst out, "Christy, have you heard about Jill?"

"No. What about her?" The mention of Jill Rogers' name put a few butterflies in my stomach as always, and I was mad at myself because of it. Forgetting that Jill had been Mike's girl once seemed to be an impossible task for me.

"Brace yourself!" Betsy sounded breathless. "You won't believe this!"

"What is it? Don't keep me in suspense. What about Jill?"

"She has quit school."

I didn't think I'd heard Betsy correctly at first.

"Did you say *quit?*" I asked. "For keeps? Do you mean she's dropped out — and this near to graduation? Are you sure?"

"I couldn't take it in, either, Christy. Kim phoned me a couple of hours ago. She'd heard it from Bud, and he got it from Carl Browning, but then Bud went to see Jill and it's true."

Mashing the phone hard against my ear, I sat down abruptly on the den couch.

"Why?" I managed, still unsure of the truth, although I didn't doubt Kim's or Bud's information, especially if he had spoken to Jill.

"She was flunking. That's what Carl told Bud."

"That doesn't make sense, Betsy. Seniors get a second chance if they fail an exam. It's why seniors in Greenview take their exams a week before other students, to allow time to make up a bad grade."

"I know. I'm sure Jill does, too. But it must be deeper than that. And you know how she is. She never cracks a book, and I guess she realized she wouldn't get her diploma with the rest of the class even if she were to take makeup exams and pass them. Carl told Bud she said she'd have to make a full *A* on every exam to bring her report card grades up to passing, which makes me think she must have had nothing but *D*'s and *F*'s the entire semester."

"How did Carl take it?" I asked.

"Bud said he was upset and mad with her, too. Apparently he thinks it's a dumb move on her part."

"I think that, too."

"Carl also told Bud that Jill had been warned by Mr. Brady some time ago that she might not graduate if she didn't improve. That would have terrified me."

"Me, too," I agreed.

"It must not have bothered Jill. It seems she made an *F* on her term paper because she didn't bother to have footnotes, and Carl said she admitted she hadn't written but a third of her chemistry lab reports since March. Those two items would give her *F*'s in chemistry and English."

"Betsy, will Carl graduate? He couldn't have studied much more than she did, since they've been together so much."

"Carl hopes he will. Gordon told me that a while back, and Bud claims it's true. Carl is hanging in, studying all of a sudden. According to what Carl said to Bud, if he flunks he's going to summer school and will try to get his diploma by fall. He wasn't planning to go to college. Neither is Jill, for that matter, although I remember hearing her say once she'd like to take a secretarial course in a city after she finished Greenview High, and I bet a secretarial school — a good one — won't enroll her if she doesn't have a high school diploma."

The den was so quiet I heard my own breathing. The western sun filtered through the leaves of the maple tree at the corner of our house, making a pattern of lights and shadows on the rug.

"Will Jill go to summer school like Carl?" I asked.

"Apparently she doesn't plan it. Bud said she's heading for Virginia Beach — going tomorrow, in fact — to get a summer job, and when the beach season ends in September or October, she'll decide what to do next if her job doesn't carry over into the winter. Isn't it unbelievable?"

"Yes. I can't take it in. To be this close to graduation and then to quit. . . . It boggles my mind."

"I feel the same way, Christy." She waited a moment and said, "If Mike were alive, do you suppose he could talk her out of leaving school?"

The mention of Mike made my throat go dry. He probably would have tried to talk Jill out of it, because he was that kind of person.

"Somebody should attempt to talk her out of it," I muttered.

"Bud has, but he didn't make her change her mind. He asked Kim if he should try, and Kim told him yes because he and Jill have known each other all their lives, but it was a lost cause. Jill told Bud there was nothing in Greenview for her and that her mind was made up, that she'd been thinking about it for a week. Apparently Jill's mother doesn't like the idea, but Jill is eighteen now and informed her mother she could leave home legally if she wants."

"What about her brother?" I asked. I knew Jill often baby-sat with her brother's children. "He might be able to influence her."

"Bud asked that, too. Jill said her brother thought she was acting dumb, but that didn't make her change plans."

I didn't speak at once, and after a long minute, Betsy said, "What's wrong, Christy?"

"Nothing. I'm just stunned. Look, I have to run. Mama has dinner on the table."

"Wait a sec! Are you coming to Sonny's tonight? Gordon and I are going."

"I have a date with Ralph tonight. He didn't mention any specific plans, so we'll probably be there."

I must have sat on the den couch at least fifteen minutes after she hung up, my mind whirling. The part about dinner being ready was a little white lie, but Betsy's reference to Mike had unnerved me. Would Mike have been able to influence Jill about staying in school? I didn't know, but if anybody could have talked her into changing her mind, no doubt Mike Maxwell would have been that person.

All of a sudden I found myself feeling sorry for Jill. She had beauty, and while she wasn't dumb and could have passed her courses in high school if she'd put forth any effort, all she cared about was having fun.

Tomorrow didn't concern her. She could think only of the present. I wanted pleasure, too, but that wasn't the most important part of my life. I also wanted an education and an interesting career in whatever field I chose, and, later, to get married and have children. Perhaps Jill wanted those same things as much as I did, hoping they'd fall into her lap with no effort on her part.

There was a shallow side to her despite her gorgeous figure and cute smile and her gold-flecked auburn hair. She could attract dates easily, but apparently she bored them after a while. Her beauty wasn't enough to make boys want her indefinitely.

As I sat on the den couch, it amazed me that I could see Jill for what she was and now think about her with pity instead of becoming rigid with anger at the mention of her name. I was sorry that she wasn't willing to work for her diploma even if she didn't receive it on schedule — the same reaction I would have had if any other member of the senior class walked out of school ten days before commencement. Shivering a little in the warm room, I recalled how jealous I'd been of Jill in the past and was dumbfounded at being able to feel compassion for her. Mike would have been proud of me for it, I thought.

Sixteen

My graduation day had made-to-order sunshine. The sky was a brilliant blue and the air was so clear that all the mountain ranges were visible across the horizon. It was neither hot nor cold, but a perfect in-between temperature.

We seniors rehearsed the procession and taking our places so many times that I expected it to be routine, but on the Tuesday morning that was graduation day, my heart beat abnormally fast as I put on my new white dress and, then, my cap and gown. We had to be at school an hour and a half before the program began at eleven o'clock, and Dad drove me into town.

Just before he and I left the house, he and Mama gave me my graduation gift — a lovely wristwatch. "It's beautiful," I told them. "How can I ever thank you?"

"You already have, dear. Many times," my

mother replied. "We're very proud of you."

"If you make pretty speeches like that, you'll have me crying in a minute." I looked from her to Dad.

"Watch it — no tears and that's an order," Dad said. "What time is it, Christy? Shouldn't we be on our way?"

Consulting my new watch, I announced that it was a quarter past nine and that, yes, we ought to go since I needed to be at school by nine-thirty.

At school, students were milling about the classroom where we were to assemble, everyone smiling and all of us thrilled to be wearing caps and gowns at last. I guess the other seniors were as excited as I was. Carl Browning came up to me first thing and grinned. His graduation had been in doubt until he'd taken two makeup exams and passed them.

"Hi, Christy," he said. "Big day at last — and I mean a capital *B* for *B*ig and a capital *D* for *D*ay."

"It really is," I agreed, and laughed from sheer happiness.

His smile died for a split second, and I wondered if he was thinking of Jill. Almost as a reflex, I said, "Have you heard anything from Jill since she got to the beach?"

"She has a job in a restaurant and she found a place to live in an apartment with some girls who work at the same restaurant. She sounds okay."

He seemed about to say something else and must have changed his mind. Maybe Jill wished she'd studied more during the spring or that she hadn't acted impulsively — if it was an impulse — and left town.

Those thoughts were interrupted when Ralph joined me as Carl left to speak to somebody else, and a moment later Kim, looking anxious, came over to where I was standing and said, "Have you seen Bud, Christy? Don't tell me he overslept today of all days."

"Right here," a familiar voice answered behind her. Bud put his hands on her shoulders, turning her around to face him. "But you keep on worrying about me, Kim, will you? I like that a lot."

Everyone in hearing laughed at Kim's consternation, and I saw the tender glances she exchanged with Bud. They truly were in love. Betsy and Gordon joined the group, and then Nina arrived.

Nina motioned me to one side. "Guess what, Christy?" she asked in an excited whisper. "My dad is here to see me graduate!" She had never looked more beautiful or happier.

"All the way from California?" I asked. "Did you know he was coming?"

"Not until our doorbell rang late yesterday afternoon. But my mother knew. Dad phoned Mom a week ago and said he'd like to be here but wouldn't come if she thought it would upset me. *Upset me?* Can you take that in? You know, I'm anything but upset unless that's a new synonym for *thrilled*. Dad didn't bring his wife, either. That would have been awkward for Mom — maybe awkward for me, too, although I've met her and my mother hasn't. Anyway, he said she came East as far as Chicago on the plane with him and is visiting friends there. He'll meet her at O'Hare Field tonight and they'll go back to California together."

"Then he won't be here long?"

"Just a few hours, but" — she beamed as she spoke — "his coming is what matters. He took Mom and me out to dinner last night before he went back to the motel where he's staying, and he'll leave Greenview this afternoon. He flew into Roanoke yesterday and rented a car to drive here, and he'll head for Roanoke Airport again after lunch. Oh, Christy, I know Dad really loves me! Of course, I always *thought* he did and he's been great whenever I've seen him since the divorce, and he sends Mom money for me regularly, but this is proof. I never would have dared hope he'd come all the way from the West Coast just to see me get my dipl —"

Mrs. Perkins, my homeroom teacher who was senior class advisor, rapped on a desk to get everyone's attention. Nina stopped talking in the middle of the sentence.

"It's time to line up," Mrs. Perkins announced. "You know your proper places, and please stay in alphabetical order or you won't receive the correct diplomas and you'll have to endure a horrible exchange later. No talking from now on, and remember that when

I give the signal for you to march, everybody should start on his or her left foot, so you'll be in step. Congratulations and good luck."

The school band, which was seated to the right of the stage, struck up "Pomp and Circumstance." Like the others in line, I thrust my left foot forward. We seniors came from the school building in a single file and crossed the paved parking lot to reach the athletic field.

The people on stage stood up and so did the crowd in the bleachers. I was amazed at the size of the audience, although Betsy had told me in advance that the town turned out for commencement whenever the weather was good. My parents were there, but I couldn't pick them out amid so many faces.

The music continued until the last senior was in place. *This is it,* I thought. *I'm actually graduating.* It was almost like watching a movie, because I was part of everything happening around me and yet detached, alone in a throng of people. It seemed unreal.

Mr. Brady introduced the dignitaries on the platform to the audience and the senator made his address, telling the class to be true to its ideals and to take pride in being worthy of our country.

Awarding diplomas was next, but before that happened there was one event not listed on the printed program. Mr. Brady announced that Matthew Dunne, president of the senior class, had asked to be allowed to make a few remarks.

I was surprised, wondering what in the world Matthew would say, but when I turned my head to glance at my classmates on either side of me, the others didn't appear as stunned as I was. Matthew left his seat and walked up the short flight of steps leading to the stage, the sunshine glinting on his yellow hair. I'd never seen him as solemn as he was then.

"Members of the school board, Mr. Brady and other faculty members, parents and friends," he began, "I am not speaking just for myself, but for every member of the graduating class when I remind you that one senior who should have been here is not with us today. Mike Maxwell died last January, and our class feels it would be wrong not to mention Mike."

A lump rose into my throat and I swallowed hard to make it go away, but it failed to move. There was absolute silence on the athletic field as Matthew paused. I was hot and cold all at once. Then, without realizing what was happening, I had myself under control. I felt a calmness, almost as though Mike had stretched out his hand to me. Maybe the mountains had something to do with it . . . and the beautiful weather . . . Mike's mountains and Mike's kind of day. Lifting my head, sitting tall in my chair, I focused my eyes on Matthew and waited for what he had to say.

"Mike Maxwell was an exceptional person," Matthew continued. "He had more friends than anybody I've ever known, because he was a friend to everyone. He was always the first to lend a hand to help people who needed help, and his death was a tragedy that has left permanent scars on his classmates. Until he died, I doubt if it ever occurred to any of his classmates that he wouldn't receive his diploma when the rest of us received ours."

A light breeze rippled the flag on the pole at the far end of the athletic field. It was the only sound until Matthew spoke again.

"If I could speak to Mike right now," he went on, "I'd tell him an important truth. I'd say, 'Mike, all of us wish you were here, but perhaps you'd like to know that your life, even though it was short, touched each of our lives. We're very glad to have had the opportunity to have known you.'"

For a minute, there was silence as Matthew left the stage, and in the next minute everyone was clapping — everyone but me. I couldn't. My heart was too full for that, although I realized I was smiling. I felt lucky. I had known Mike better than almost anyone else, and I'd been fortunate enough to have his love. Sitting there on the athletic field with the sunshine warm across my shoulders, I was surprisingly dry-eyed.

Mr. Brady began to speak again, and I forced my attention to the platform. The seniors rose in a body, and, as he called the names, one by one we marched across the grass to the steps and onto the stage where

163

the chairman of the school board handed out diplomas.

It seemed forever to reach the J's. Kim and Betsy, whose last names began with the leter C, had their diplomas and were back in their seats before I began the slow walk across the stage. Gordon Sager would come later. and Bud Warren was always near the end of any alphabetical line. I managed to murmur, "Thank you," as the rolled-up parchment was placed in my hand. Like the others, I walked to the opposite side of the stage and went down a second set of steps to my seat.

And then it was over.

The band was playing once more, a happy-go-lucky march instead of the serious processional, and the seniors were hugging each other, all of us jabbering at once. Matthew came to my side and put his mouth close to my ear. "Christy," he said, "everybody knew about the eulogy to Mike except you. It wasn't mentioned in a formal class meeting but it was agreed that we wanted to recognize him in public. I was afraid you might get upset if you found out in advance and not be able to enjoy graduation."

"It was wonderful, Matthew." I smiled at him. "You said it perfectly. Mike would have liked it and liked being remembered."

Bud, with one arm around Kim, put his other arm around me. "We made it!" he said, and Ralph echoed the same happy thought. My reply to both of them was lost in the hubbub of laughter and chatter, as the people who'd been in the bleachers spilled down to the athletic field.

Parents and seniors found each other; I saw Mama and Dad at last. They smiled just as I was smiling, and, as they came toward me, I saw someone else important to me coming across the athletic field, taking long strides. David Webster. He hurried in my direction, his smile as wide as mine, and he reached me before my parents did.

"I thought you had to work today, David!" I gasped. He'd told me he would be on duty.

"Why do you think I've slaved the last two weekends? It was so I could have today off. I didn't mention it because I wanted to surprise you."

"It's a surprise. A marvelous one."

"You don't mind my coming, do you?"

"Are you kidding? Mind? I'm thrilled." I laughed as I spoke, recalling how Nina had made a similar statement a short time earlier.

"I don't know what plans you have for the rest of today, Christy," David said, "but I've fixed a picnic lunch for us if you're free and —"

Betsy and Gordon put in an appearance, and David hushed. But he grinned at them and murmured, "Congratulations."

"Christy, I've decided to have a crowd at my house tonight. It's a spur-of-the-moment deal and won't be fancy, but I hope you and David will come." She turned to him. "Graduation is probably old stuff to you, but it's new to us. You can help the rest of us celebrate."

"Sure. I'll be there," he grinned. "That is, if Christy will come with me."

"Just try and stop me," I said.

As Betsy and Gordon moved from us I looked at David. "What were you saying about a picnic?" I asked.

"I had this picnic brainstorm this morning when I woke up and saw what a beautiful day it is. Phoned Lee Carlyle to ask if he and Nina would like to come with us, but he told me Nina's father had come and besides, Lee is having exams. He asked if you and I would like to use his father's farm, where we went before. You can bet I said yes in a hurry."

"David, that sounds great, but I'll have to go home and change."

"Me, too. You don't think I'm going to picnic in a coat and tie, do you? Suppose I drive you to your house, and, after you change, we can stop by my place for me to get into jeans and grab the lunch. I really have made sandwiches. Honest. I hope you go for peanut butter and jelly because that's what I happened to have on hand."

"My favorite kind."

"A woman after my own heart. I knew you were the type to appreciate gourmet food." He pretended to be serious, but we looked into each other's eyes and smiled again.

Mama and Dad apparently had seen David talking to me and they'd held back. I found

them and went to them, mentioning the picnic plans as well as the gathering at Betsy's
house for later. I knew my mother well
enough to realize she had been afraid I would
be tense after Matthew's tribute to Mike, and
now, she was relieved to see that I wasn't.
She squeezed my hand in an understanding
gesture, while Dad, teasing me, said, "Do
I have to call you Miss Jamison now that
you're a graduate, Christy?"

"I'll have to think about that," I told him,
and laughed. He laughed, too.

David and I didn't talk much on the way
to my house. As he turned from the highway
into the lane leading up our hill, I said, "It
won't take me long to change clothes, David.
I really am a fast dresser, so wait in the car
or come in the house, whichever you want."

"It's such a nice day I'll stay outside. But
before you go in, I have something for you."
Cutting off the car engine, he reached into
the side pocket of his coat for a small, tissue-
wrapped box that he handed to me. "That's
because you just graduated."

I removed the paper and ribbon, finding a
bottle of my favorite perfume.

"David, it's wonderful. Thanks loads —
for the gift and for thinking of me."

"It's easy to think about you. I do it when
I ought to be thinking about other matters.
Wait — don't leave yet. I have something
else, something you can use in Charlottesville
next fall."

167

I hadn't noticed the box on the backseat, as he'd hidden it under a newspaper. This package was much larger than the perfume, and I unwrapped it to find a dark blue loose-leaf notebook with UNIVERSITY OF VIRGINIA in gold letters at the top, and, in the same gold letters only a smaller size, my name, CHRISTY JAMISON, embossed in the lower right-hand corner.

"Oh, David . . . I'm speechless. First the perfume, and now this. I'll enjoy both of them."

"And think of me whenever you use either?"

"Of course."

When I met his eyes, the smoky look was in them and his smile was tender. He didn't say he was going to kiss me. He simply did it, and the kiss was as dear as I knew it would be.

I hung my white dress in the closet and put on jeans and my favorite yellow knitted shirt, humming softly. Everything about the morning had been perfect — the program, having my diploma, the love and pride in my parents' faces, the mention of Mike, and now, David's gifts and the picnic plans.

Betsy had invited David to her party as casually as if he, too, were a member of the graduating class, and he appeared pleased when he accepted. I knew everything would be fine, that he wouldn't be stiff and that my friends would accept him.

The summer stretched out ahead. Mr. Carlyle had asked me to work a couple of days a week at the gift shop until the middle of July, when he expected his business to slack off, and the timing was perfect. The end of every July my family went to visit relatives in Indiana in the small town where both Mama and Dad were born, and as soon as we were home again, it would be less than a month before I'd be leaving for college. I'd have plenty of getting ready to do, and, best of all, leaving for Charlottesville wouldn't mean I'd be telling David good-bye, since he'd be in school there, too.

"Hey, fast dresser!" David called from the yard. "How much longer?"

Going to the window in my room, I looked down at him. He was leaning against the front fender of the car, looking up.

"I thought you said you were speedy," he went on. "You've been gone five whole minutes. What's keeping you? I'm starved and if you don't hurry, I just might go on and eat every one of those peanut butter and jelly sandwiches and make you go hungry."

"I wouldn't want that to happen," I laughed. "Coming right now."

As I came out of the front door, he met me on the porch and kissed the tip of my nose. "That kiss is for coming on the double after I yelled," he grinned.

"You mean that little peck is all I rate?" I pretended to pout.

"All you rate *now*." He winked at me. "But

when we reach the picnic place, since you're a graduate, maybe you'll rate another kiss. Mind you, I'm not promising. It's a maybe."

I fell in with his teasing. "And do I have to bring my diploma?"

"I don't think so. You have 'graduation' written all over you."

I looked upset. "But I want to have 'college' written all over me!"

"But first, my dear, the summer!" David finished, bowing before me and helping me toward the car.

"You are a character, David Webster," I said, and giggled. "I —"

He didn't give me a chance to finish. "Why don't we take care of that next kiss this very minute?" he asked, and his lips came down on mine. It was a long, sweet kiss, and when it ended we smiled at each other.

It was after midnight when I reached home that night. The picnic had been fun, and, in addition to laughing and kissing, David and I had talked seriously. He wasn't sure if he wanted to go into general medicine or specialize, and when he asked what sort of career I wanted, and I mentioned marketing, he nodded.

"You'll be good at that, Christy," he said. "You know how to talk to people and that's important in any field, but especially in something like marketing."

"You know how to talk to people, too,"

I told him. "At least, you can get through to me."

"Remarks like that will send you to the top of the class," he came back, and we laughed together.

At Betsy's, my friends welcomed him and he appeared at ease, obviously having a good time. That made the party double fun for me, and so we lingered until everyone else was leaving.

I thought about all of it as I undressed, after kissing David good-night and watching him drive down the hill. The bedside lamp was on in my room, casting a faint glow, and almost from force of habit I went to the chest of drawers and picked up Mike's picture.

I didn't talk to Mike, just looked at the snapshot, and then I did something unexpected. Instead of returning the picture to the top of the chest of drawers, I tucked it into a drawer. At that instant I knew that at last I could think about Mike Maxwell rationally. It wasn't that I was forgetting him — I could never do that even if I'd wanted to do it — but I realized that he was a part of my life that was over. My future lay ahead, with the prospect of meeting new people and doing interesting things. Mike couldn't be an active part of my future, even though he would always be vital to me.

My mind was jammed with exciting thoughts as I crawled into bed. David . . . graduation . . . the summer . . . college . . . David. . . . I smiled to myself in the darkness.

WILDFIRE.

Move from one breathtaking romance to another with the #1 Teen Romance line in the country!

NEW WILDFIRES! $1.95 each

- ☐ MU32539-6 **BLIND DATE** Priscilla Maynard
- ☐ MU32541-8 **NO BOYS?** McClure Jones
- ☐ MU32538-8 **SPRING LOVE** Jennifer Sarasin
- ☐ MU31930-2 **THAT OTHER GIRL** Conrad Nowels

BEST-SELLING WILDFIRES! $1.95 each

- ☐ MU31981-7 **NANCY AND NICK** Caroline B. Cooney
- ☐ MU32313-X **SECOND BEST** Helen Cavanagh
- ☐ MU31849-7 **YOURS TRULY, LOVE, JANIE** Ann Reit
- ☐ MU31566-8 **DREAMS CAN COME TRUE** Jane Claypool Miner
- ☐ MU32369-5 **HOMECOMING QUEEN** Winifred Madison
- ☐ MU31261-8 **I'M CHRISTY** Maud Johnson
- ☐ MU30324-4 **I'VE GOT A CRUSH ON YOU** Carol Stanley
- ☐ MU32361-X **THE SEARCHING HEART** Barbara Steiner
- ☐ MU31710-5 **TOO YOUNG TO KNOW** Elisabeth Ogilvie
- ☐ MU32430-6 **WRITE EVERY DAY** Janet Quin-Harkin
- ☐ MU30956-0 **THE BEST OF FRIENDS** Jill Ross Klevin